# A SNOWMAN MADE OF SAND

## AND SIX OTHER SWEET ROMANCE SHORT STORIES

## STEPHANNIE TALLENT

*To Dave, who loves my sweet romances the best*

# CONTENTS

# A SNOWMAN MADE OF SAND

No matter how many tree lighting ceremonies on various small town Southern Californian piers and plazas, no matter how loud the Christmas music in the upscale outdoor mall up on the hill in Palos Verdes, or how pungent the piped-in scent of pine trees it seemed was *everywhere*, it just didn't feel like Christmas to Eliza.

Maybe it was the sun glittering on the blue Pacific waves dotted with surfers in sleek black wetsuits, or the sunny, balmy seventy-degree weather, or the tourists still wading into the surf in flip flops and cargo shorts, squealing at the cold bite of the water as the waves slapped at their shins.

Or maybe, it was just that Los Angeles wasn't home.

Five months ago, she'd taken the job at Orbital Unlimited. She'd turned down Boeing, Northrop, even SpaceX, for the job. It had sounded like a dream come true, the potential to have her own team within a year. Everything she'd worked so hard for, graduating near the top of her class at Yale with a joint degree in Astrophysics and Computer Science, then to MIT for her doctorate.

All the long nights and early mornings in New Haven. All the skipped romances and parties and things that made college, well, college, even if it was a top notch school chock full of ambitious students.

The car wreck, taking away her parents right before grad school, also took away any reason to go back to Saint Charles, Illinois, where they'd moved after Eliza finished high school. She'd so loved visiting them at Christmas, window shopping in the quaint downtown area, hiking together along the Fox River in snow boots and a parka. Playing board games, from Scrabble to Catan, plus whatever special new games her dad found, pouring over online review sites.

Then, all the lonely Christmas breaks these past four years, with days and nights spent in the Barker Library at MIT at a table under its big dome, sunlight or moonlight shining through the center oculus, backlit columns aligned along the walls, studying, researching.

She would steal just a few moments at midnight for herself, tromping through fresh fallen powder, *shusharrah* squeaks under her waterproof, rubber soled boots, crisp air tight in her lungs. She always loved her solitary winter walks from the neoclassical library to her un-renovated, shabby brownstone apartment. On those nights, she didn't even mind climbing up the three flights of creaking stairs to her top floor studio, or the building's temperamental furnace. She would just curl up under her down comforter, falling asleep to the soft glow of lights on her little Christmas tree.

By morning the snowfall would be packed and gray, if not more suspicious colors, but she loved the fresh snow.

Her building had a tiny backyard, just a dirt lot filled with weeds in the summertime. Every year at Christmas break, after enough snow had accumulated and buried all the dried weeds, she'd make a small snowman, just for herself.

That last fall, when the leaves turned bright vibrant orange and scarlet and yellow, she'd started interviewing at different aerospace companies. Her advisor, Dr Lacey Jacobs, encouraged her to do a post doc, with an eye towards academia, but Eliza wanted to do hands-on, practical research and projects.

All the aerospace companies were eager to hire talented women; Orbits Unlimited more so than the others.

The company romanced her with the South Bay Los Angeles techie version of wining and dining. Mark from HR and some of the other guys took her out to local breweries featuring Hazy IPAs, fruit infused Saisons, and barrel aged Imperial stouts, with names that cleverly referenced physics and engineering. They introduced her to restaurants in nearby trendy Manhattan Beach, feeding her pasta with rich roasted bone marrow at one restaurant, flaky cheddar bacon biscuits at another, and more takes on sushi than she knew what to think of.

She was so overwhelmed and excited she didn't even notice she'd be the only female engineer, and what that said about the culture at Orbital, and why they were so eager to hire a woman.

That winter, her backyard snowman sported a blue and orange striped plywood surfboard and dark sunglasses.

AND HERE SHE WAS, leaning against the salt-stained wooden railing at the end of the Hermosa Beach pier, a wary eye out for the weekend fishermen casting off the pier all around her, her long curly red hair whipping around her face in the stiff breeze. She inhaled the briny air, tasting the saltiness over her cinnamon flavored lip balm, watching the sun glitter off the ocean.

In December. Wearing saddle tanned strappy sandals, white t-shirt knotted at her flat belly, and faded cut off jeans, and reeking of coconut sunscreen. In *December*.

Two weekends ago she'd learned her fair skin would burn bright red even in the low winter sunlight: the joys of being a redhead of Irish descent.

She caught a glimpse of one rounded dorsal fin rolling in and out of the water, then another, then one more, just thirty yards away. A pod of dolphins! She smiled. So sleek and fast and free. Seeing dolphins always raised her spirits.

But then she thought of work again. Of being shut out of the big contracts. Once Orbital got her, and she had uprooted herself from the East Coast, it was like they had no clue what to do with her.

Treat her the same as the men, darn it!

Dr Jacobs had tried to warn her of the bro culture at so many of the tech firms. She hadn't had the opportunity to form any friendships here; after work, her unmarried peers took off in groups to those same breweries, ignoring her, and the rare married ones went home straight away to their wives (totally understandable).

Most of the secretaries and receptionists, almost all women, viewed her with suspicion. She wasn't one of them. She was an engineer.

She'd overheard too many snide comments from the guys about her being hired as the token female engineer (but at least hot). She'd walked into too many meetings, expecting the discussion to be about the project, and interrupted crude jokes that trailed off at her entrance, and started up when she left.

Management kept shuttling her from minor project to minor project, so she never had a chance to follow through on any of her ideas, or to even gain any support from her fellow engineers. She wasn't incompetent, but that was how she was beginning to feel.

High cirrus clouds scudded across the sun, graying out the sky and dropping the temperature ten degrees. Eliza shivered. Sometimes it did feel like winter, even in Los Angeles.

COFFEE. Coffee and caffeine always helped.

She'd noticed a new coffeehouse, Bean and Board, up the street from the pier, in a renovated single-story wood-sided beach cottage.

She decided to try it. She'd walk right by it on the way to her car, anyways.

The cottage had been painted a bright cheery yellow with white trim. The scent of cinnamon coffee cake and rich dark coffee wafted out of the wedged-open front door.

Her stomach growled. She loved cinnamon on anything.

She went in. The space was wide open; obviously some walls had been knocked down during the renovation. The oak floors looked original, a bit warped and beat up, but were polished to a soft warm glow. Hung on the white-painted shiplap walls were vintage longboards, some waxed to warm yellow wooden tones, others coated with bright resins, mint green and sky blue and warm red. Colorful Christmas lights festooned each longboard, reflections twinkling off the soft sheen of the boards. Photos of surfers, flat white picture frames setting off the blues of the waves and the colorful fiberglass-sheathed shortboards, were interspersed between the longboards.

A thickly cushioned cream canvas futon with red and white striped pillows sat against the back wall, its flat, unfinished pine arms broad enough to serve as end tables for a small plate with a cookie or for a mug of coffee. Knock off lacquered bent plywood Eames-style chairs around bistro tables made of recycled surfboards filled the center of the room. Several were taken by patrons, sipping espresso and munching on pastries, working on their Macs. A long, reclaimed-wood table, big enough to seat at least sixteen, was along the wall to her left. Backless benches provided seating for it.

To her right was a black laminate counter with a sleek tablet terminal as a register and a glass case full of pastries (including the coffee cake!). A sleek Italian espresso machine stretched across a second counter against the wall, along with a heavy duty grinder.

Above the espresso machine was a chalkboard menu: coffee drinks, pastries, even sandwiches. The mozzarella and heirloom tomato sandwich sounded tasty.

"What can I get you?" the barista asked.

Eliza looked up. And up. *You!* she thought. She could feel her face flush beet red.

He was tanned, with sun-streaked brown hair pulled back in a short pony tail. Broad shoulders filled a faded blue Billabong-emblazoned t-shirt, and baggy khaki shorts managed somehow to accentuate his trim waist. The bottom of a tattoo peeked out from beneath his right sleeve. And tall! Eliza was short at 5'2", but he was at least a foot taller.

He was maybe a few years older than her, in his early thirties. Small crinkles at the corners of his eyes spoke to lots of time in the sun and water. He looked a little like a young Sam Shepherd. *The Right Stuff* was one of her favorite movies *ever*.

And those eyes ... she could fall into his gorgeous bright brown eyes forever.

They were the improbable color of cinnamon.

Cinnamon.

She was surrounded by guys at work, and not one had affected her this way, even before she realized most were jerks.

"Um," she said, then rallied. "A latte? Two shots, whole milk? And a piece of that coffee cake?"

"For here, or to go?" His voice was as rich and tasty as cinnamon, too.

"To go," she squeaked.

"Want that cake warmed up?"

Oh boy did she ever. "Yes, please." She tried to pull herself together, to say something intelligent. "How long have you guys been open?"

"Just a week since last Sunday. Crazy time of the year to open, I know, but the property became available a couple months ago and I didn't want to risk losing it. Jake," he said, sticking his hand out across the counter.

"Eliza." His grip was warm and strong; not enough to hurt, but enough to show her he respected her. Or at least that's how she interpreted it. "The place looks great. I bet you'll do great."

"Thanks," he said. "Hope so. Here's a frequent flyer card. Buy ten drinks, get the next one free." He punched the card, smiled at her, then did nine more punches. "Just want to make sure you come back." He handed it back to her, his fingers brushing hers. No rings.

Engineers do *not* swoon in coffee shops.

She fidgeted while he made her latte and warmed up the cake, looking everywhere but at him. Except for sidelong glances she couldn't help.

He placed her items on the counter. "Sugar, cocoa powder, napkins etc are over there." Jake gestured to a table off to the side, set up with various coffee accoutrements. "Hey, I don't know if you like board games, but I'm hosting—well, the coffee shop is—game nights on Tuesdays. You should come. 7 p.m. Redeem that free latte."

"Thanks," Eliza said. "I will."

JAKE WATCHED the young woman leave. Cute as a button, with all that curly red hair and bright green eyes. A little awkward, but sweet. He really hoped she'd come back on Tuesday. His sister Kathy would be running the counter, freeing him up to have some fun playing board games. He'd barely had any time off for the last couple months, getting Bean and Board up and running.

And it'd been longer than that since he'd met a girl he wanted to see more than once. Since that nasty break up with Ashley.

Yes, he was looking forward to Tuesday night.

MONDAY MORNING, back to work. Eliza carefully parked her cherry red Miata, a gift to herself for landing the Orbital job, in the corner of the lot furthest from the entrance. So far it didn't have any dings, and she wanted to keep it that way.

Orbital Unlimited, headquartered in El Segundo, just south of the Los Angeles airport, operated out of a newly built modern building. Constructed of thick concrete slabs and immense glass panes, the building sprawled, taking up half the city block. The interior was half computer and other laboratories, half office space and conference rooms. It did have a coffee bar and lounge downstairs, along with old-school stand up video arcade games like Galaga and Pac-Man, for when the teams needed a break.

"Hi, Shelly," Eliza greeted the receptionist, who was typing away at her keyboard at her sleek curved desk in the terrazzo-floored entryway.

Shelly glanced up, pushing her thick, blond-streaked hair out of her sharp featured, tanned face. "Message from the boss," she said. "Mike wants to see you as soon you get in." She went back to typing.

Eliza stood still, unsure. Did that mean after she at least dropped off her messenger bag at her desk?

"Now," said Shelly, not even looking up. "He's in his office."

Eliza went straight there, mind buzzing in worry. She had double checked all her numbers and coding on the last simulation, checking re-entry stability for a prototype sub-orbital small passenger ship.

She knew she hadn't made any mistakes. Her work was nearly always perfect, to the grudging acknowledgement of the other engineers.

"Come in," Mike said as she knocked on the doorframe to his glassed-in office. He was reviewing reports at his desk, a teak and steel Mad Men monstrosity. Two Herman Miller ivory leather office chairs sat in front of the desk. From the full length windows behind it he had a peek view of the tree-filled acreage of the adjacent refinery after which the town was named: El Segundo, The Second, location of the second Standard Oil refinery in California.

Mike was older that most of the engineers; even so, she gauged him to be in his early 40s, not any older, with a round, clean shaven face, cold blue eyes, and dark hair just starting to thin on top. She was a little nervous around him. He was one of the cofounders of the company.

He didn't offer for her to sit.

Or mince words.

"Eliza, we're letting you go. It's just not working out. We've tried you with different teams, and the guys just say you don't gel with any of them. It's not your work, just the team aspect. Mark from HR has a severance package for you, so go see him next. No hard feelings." He nodded to her, dismissing her, looking back down at the reports.

She stood there, stunned, her face warming to that beet red color she just couldn't suppress. *She* didn't gel? She didn't even have the chance! "Sir, respectfully, your guys shut me out of everything and ignored all my suggestions. No one would even leave me with one team long enough for me to become part of it."

He glanced up. "Perhaps," he said, "if you'd been more forceful earlier, things may've been different."

"You're blaming *me*?" She couldn't even. The gall. The unfairness. She turned and walked out, kicking aside the door stop wedging open his door and grabbing the edge of the glass door just so she could slam it. She'd show him forceful.

Going to HR would mean walking through the open office space on the second floor. If Shelly, a vicious gossip behind that sleek snooty exterior, knew Eliza was being fired, everyone else did too.

Screw them. She had to collect her things, anyways. Not that she kept much at the office that was personal.

No one met her eyes as she packed up, or as she signed paperwork with Mark in HR, or as she stomped out past Shelly, who openly gawked as her. *Screw* them.

Merry freakin' Christmas.

She peeled out of the parking lot and drove home.

HOME WAS a small 1920s Spanish bungalow she rented in South Redondo Beach on an alphabet street: Avenue E, to be precise, with a sneak peek of the Pacific from her front deck. The front yard was landscaped with native plants, from aromatic sages that, when damp with dew or fog or rain, perfumed the morning air with their wild scent, to *Ceanothus* with glossy green leaves and, when in bloom, vibrant lilac flowers. Fruit trees, Eureka and Meyer lemons, Key and Persian limes, shaded the small fenced backyard, with its gravel-covered ground and fairy lights twinkling off the back deck.

She'd love to buy a home like it someday, creaking original floors and banged up plaster and all. Maybe even *this* home. Get a dog. Something soft and fluffy with floppy ears, that would curl up with her on the couch and cuddle.

She could use some cuddling right now.

Her thoughts flashed to Jake at the coffee shop.

Nope, not now. Focus on getting out a resume. The severance package was very generous, enough that she wondered if she might've had a sexual harassment case. All those crude jokes. Regardless, she had enough money, between the severance and savings, to not rush into another bad fit. But it didn't mean she could put off a job search for months, either.

She tweaked her resume, then emailed Dr Jacobs. She wanted to call, but she knew it was Christmas break at MIT.

Yes. It *was* Christmas time. And as hurt and furious as she was, maybe losing this job, that she hated anyways, was a gift. Of sorts.

She hadn't even felt up to getting a tree. Even in Boston she'd always put up a table-top sized tree, and decorated it with ornaments she'd inherited from her parents. Those ornaments were neatly packed up in boxes on the top shelf in the closet of the spare bedroom.

This year, she hadn't wanted to get a tree. Now she did, darn it. She tossed an old sheet into her car, put the top down, then drove back up Pacific Coast Highway, PCH, to the Kiwanis tree lot in Hermosa Beach. She'd read their banner on her drive home this morning, driving from El Segundo through Manhattan Beach and Hermosa, then to Redondo: *All Proceeds to Local Charities*. Sounded good to her.

The lot smelled like pine trees, real pine trees, not fake piped in smells. She picked out a six foot Noble fir, with nice even branches, enough room between them to showcase her ornaments, but not so much it looked skimpy. She added a tree stand and four packages of white lights; then, biting her lip, added two more packages, to string along her front porch railing. Go all out, Eliza!

One of the guys at the lot helped her get the tree, all wrapped up in the old sheet, into her front seat. She handed him a five dollar tip. "Thank you."

"Looks like you picked out a good one," someone said behind her.

She squeaked and jumped. *Way to look dignified!*

Jake smiled at her. Oh, those eyes. Spicy warm cinnamon. "Eliza, right? Want to help me pick one out for the coffee shop?" he asked. "Kathy usually helps me pick out a tree, but she's at the Bean."

The *yes* died on her lips. "I have to get my tree home," she said. "They just trimmed the end, I have to get it into the stand and water it."

Were those eyes disappointed? She didn't know. Kathy, huh?

"Well, you are coming tomorrow for game night, right? You need to get your free latte." He smiled. "I really hope you do."

She glanced up at him.

"We need all the players we can get," he continued.

Good lord. Her emotions couldn't take this. "Gotta go," she said.

"7 p.m. See you tomorrow," he said, as she hopped into the Miata and backed out.

TUESDAY SHE GOT UP EARLY to go for a run on the Strand, the concrete path that ran the length of the Santa Monica bay, all the way from Rat Beach in Torrance (*Right After Torrance*; she finally had to ask someone why a perfectly nice beach was named after rats!) to Will Rogers State Beach out in Pacific Palisades. She'd ridden her bike along the whole forty odd miles there and back a couple times in the summer, dodging clueless tourists nearly the entire way.

There were a couple spots in Playa del Rey and Marina del Rey where the Strand wasn't continuous. The first time she rode her bike she had gotten a little lost.

She was only planning on running from her house to Hermosa Pier and back, though. Round trip that would still be about eight miles. She needed the run to burn off her lingering anger from yesterday.

And maybe she could take a break near the Pier and grab a coffee at Bean and Board. Even if there was a Kathy in the picture, she could still look, right?

And Jake made darn good coffee.

Running shorts, tank top, cap with her pony tail pulled through, and sunscreen. Lots of sunscreen. Waist belt for a water bottle, and a zipped pouch for her keys and some cash. Ready to go. She took off running at an easy clip.

Less that forty minutes later, she was breathing a bit harder and walking into the Bean.

Jake wasn't at the counter.

A woman was. Pretty, with long dark hair and warm brown eyes, and a quick smile. "Hi!" she said. "Welcome to Bean and Board. Is this your first time?"

"Um," Eliza said. This must be Kathy. Her heart sank. She was so pretty. And nice. "Second time."

"Awesome, a repeat customer!" Kathy said. "Fantastic. We must be doing something right." She grinned. "You must've met Jake last time? I'm Kathy, his big sister."

Sister!

"And I know he's super cute, but," she leaned forward on the counter top, "I make way better coffee. Don't tell him that."

"I'm coming for game night tonight," Eliza said. "That's still on, right?"

"You bet. 7 p.m. But come a little early if you want to help pick out some games. You're Eliza, right? Jake mentioned you. Can't miss that glorious hair of yours." Kathy swiped some imaginary crumbs off the counter. "But don't tell him I said that, either. Coffee?"

"Latte, please, a double. Whole milk." Eliza smiled.

This was turning into the best week *ever*.

6:30 P.M. and Eliza was back at Bean and Board. It was already dark out, and Jake and Kathy had Christmas lights along the roof and windows of the cottage, giving it a cheery festive glow. She could see a decorated and lit Christmas tree through the front window. The smell of cinnamon coffee cake, fresh coffee, and eggnog enveloped her as she walked up.

She was wearing a bit of makeup that accentuated her bright green eyes, and her favorite jeans that fit her snugly in all the right places, along with a navy cotton Aran sweater Dr Jacobs, Lacey, had knit for her when Eliza told her she was moving to Los Angeles. Cotton, not wool, but Lacey said it did get chilly in the evenings, from what she remembered from a long ago trip to Catalina. A thick cozy sweater would be welcome. Blue suede loafers with a rubber soul completed her outfit.

Eliza's curly red hair floofed around her face and down her back, a nimbus of cheer.

Kathy was at the counter, helping a customer, when Eliza walked in. Smiling, she gave Eliza a quick thumbs up. Eliza thought she mouthed "You go, girl!" but she wasn't sure.

Eliza waved hello, then headed back to the long table off to the left. As she expected, that was the site for game night. Jake was there, looking scrumptious in faded jeans, olive green khaki sneakers, and an atrocious ugly Christmas sweater featuring reindeer, an abominable snowman, and a Tyrannosaurus with a Santa cap. He was sorting through a stack of colorful boxes: Catan, Ticket to Ride, Pandemic, and some others she didn't recognize.

"Need help?" she asked.

"Eliza! I'm so glad you made it," Jake said, eyes lighting up.

"I needed something fun to look forward to," she said. "Lost my job yesterday."

"Oh, no," he said. "Are you okay?"

She thought for a moment. "Actually, yes, I am. I was over at Orbital, and I hated it. I should've left on my own months ago, but I thought I could make it work. I'm not used to not being able to make things work."

"So you're a rocket scientist?" he said.

She blushed. "Basically, yes." She watched him beneath her lashes. If he was going to be intimidated, it would be now.

"Awesome," he said. "I had a great Physics teacher in high school, Ms Nolan. I wish I had more aptitude for it myself. Majored in English Lit and surfing at Santa Cruz, and look where I am now."

"You're doing fine," Kathy called from the counter.

Jake rolled his eyes. "Typical pushy big sister. So where are you from originally?"

"Chicago area," she said. "Then east coast, Yale and MIT. I moved out here last spring for the job."

"Oooh, fancy," he teased. "Must've been culture shock for you, though, moving out west."

She nodded. "I miss the seasons. And I miss the snow. I used to make a snowman, each Christmas break, in my backyard in Boston." Suddenly, she could feel herself tearing up. She missed her research, Lacey, and, most of all, her parents.

"Oh, sweetheart," Jake said, walking around the table to her, gathering her up in his arms.

She tensed, then let herself relax against him, burying her face in that godawful sweater, sobbing. She hoped she didn't smear mascara on it.

With her luck she would. All over the ridiculously cheery Tyrannosaur.

He stroked her hair and murmured nonsense to her. Finally, after a long couple minutes, she straightened, dashing at her eyes. "I'm so sorry," she said.

"You don't ever have to apologize to me," he said, tilting her chin up to meet her eyes. His cinnamon eyes were soft, concerned. "But hold on. Sit here, I'll be back in a few. I'll have Kathy make you a latte. Whole milk, two shots, right?"

"Yes," she said. "Thanks." She plopped down on the bench, watching him stop to talk to Kathy briefly, then head back into the kitchen. He came out, carrying a small paper bag, with a rolled up blue and red beach towel tucked under his arm, just as Kathy finished making her latte.

"Come on," he said, handing her the latte in a to-go cup and grabbing her other hand. "Kathy will start up game night. Some friends of ours promised to show up for it, so if we're a little late, it's okay."

"Where are we going?"

"Just to the beach. I need to show you something."

~

THEY WALKED DOWN to the hard packed sand at the ocean's edge, trudging first through the loose sand, getting grains stuck in their shoes. Eliza had to take off her suede loafers; the sand in her shoes was driving her nuts, but unfortunately that meant she had to let go of Jake's hand.

He spread the beach towel on the soft, dry sand just shy of the damp hard pack. "Give me ten minutes, okay?" he asked. She nodded, sitting back on the towel, wedging her latte into the sand next to her.

She could feel a the mist of ocean spray from the waves slapping against the shore. Tide was going out. Bioluminescent plankton colored the waves a soft aqua in the moonlight. The brininess was strong, pungent, crisp in the cool December air.

Jake was mounding up piles of wet sand into what looked like ... a snowman? A rather awkward, small, slumping snowman, about two feet tall, but yes, something that did look sort of like a snowman. He pulled two burnt cookies from the paper bag and stuck them onto the face (or, more precisely, what he must have intended to be the face) for eyes, then held out the bag to her.

"Your turn," he said.

She reached in, pulled out a carrot, and laughed. She stuck it into the sandy face, below the cookie eyes.

He reached an arm out, and she tucked back under it, against his warm body. He tentatively, gently, kissed the top of her head. "It's not exactly a snowman," he said. "But it's the best I can do on very short notice."

"It's perfect," Eliza said, her heart soaring.

All of a sudden, it did feel like Christmas.

# LOVE IN THE TIME OF COVID-19

*L*issa bumped open the front door to the Streamline Moderne duplex with her hip. She could see her older brother Cade, his laptop in front of him, through the dining room windows in the rounded corner of the building that jutted out.

Best room in the lower duplex for natural light, facing west with big windows. Of course Cade had set up there. She was hoping to do some knitting before bedtime. With April sun not hitting the horizon til nearly 7:30, she could knit to the sunset. Just zen out.

She missed having the upstairs duplex to herself, and the balcony she'd set up with a cheap bistro set, but last year, it had made more sense to rent it out, and she and Cade shared the bottom duplex. They had planned on using the cash from the rent to flip another of the properties inherited from their mom.

So much for *that* idea. Their upstairs tenant Randy, an actor slash waiter, couldn't really afford the rent now he was out of work, with both a lot of Hollywood and the restaurant, Osteria Ripeteri, shut down. Lissa didn't have the heart to make him pay rent. She and Cade owned the place outright, and *they* both still had their jobs.

She just hoped Randy could help with the utilities.

Onions and garlic and browned seasoned meat...Lissa swallowed.

Oh, that smelled awesome. She had worked straight through lunch at the cat clinic. Only sick pet visits were allowed, not wellness, and they'd gotten slammed today.

Maybe Randy could just cook for them, once a week, as barter. He was a kick ass amateur chef, learning as much from watching the kitchen at Osteria Ripeteri as waiting tables, and often brought them some of whatever he was experimenting with.

"Lissa, you're making dinner tonight, right?" her brother Cade asked before she even had a chance to take off her face mask, let alone change out of her cat-hair-coated scrubs. "It's time for Heavy Metal Happy Hour in a few."

Cade, a high school English Lit teacher, wore baggy khaki canvas shorts and a loose fitting plaid short sleeved shirt over a snug white t-shirt. He didn't look much different from when he was standing in front of the classroom, teaching in person rather than recording lectures at home, except at school he wore jeans, not shorts. His beach-blond hair was cut short, and his thin-rimmed reading glasses were perched near the end of his tanned nose.

Yeah, he had some tats, who didn't in LA? His peeked out from under his shirt sleeves.

*Lissa* looked more like a metalhead than aging surfer boy Cade did.

Especially now, with her mascara smudged under her eyes from sweat and tears, and her goth-black hair up in a messy ponytail. *Her* tats were full-sleeve both arms, with a Sailor Jerry mermaid with a jade green tail and lavender sea shells for a bra taking up most of her right arm and a clowder of cartoon cats, all the cats she'd had in her life so far, filling up her left.

She stomped past him to the laundry room, the old oak floors creaking underneath her. Shuck off the faded black scrubs, toss them and the cloth face mask (black cartoon cats, cute, sewn by a client) and her sports bra and underwear and socks, all of it, into the washer and set it on the *Sanitary* setting.

She pulled on a pair of black leggings and a black tank top.

Cade had a solid fifteen years on her, with Lissa being the 'oops' baby before their parents' divorce. But right now, if someone thought

Cade was the thirty-year-old and Lissa forty-five going on fifty-five, Lissa wouldn't be surprised. She felt old, old and tired and heartsick.

"Let's just order takeout," she said, plopping on the wooden ladder-back dining chair next to Cade, leaning back so she could still see the sun. The walnut dining set was as old as the 1930s duplex, but still comfortable, just like the house. "Or maybe you can text Randy to see if they want to share leftovers. From a safe social distancing distance."

"Bad day, kiddo?" he asked, looking at her, really looking at her.

"That's Doc Kiddo to you," she joked, then sobered. "Three euths. Best for the kitties, they were suffering, but god, it sucks. I couldn't even hug Mrs Bartonelli after I put Blue to sleep. I've known her and Blue since I started practicing there."

Lissa was an associate veterinarian at the Silverlake Cat Clinic, saving to buy in. One day it would be hers.

One more reason she had moved out of the upstairs duplex.

She loved the practice, the clients, and especially the cats.

But the bad went with the good. And right now there was a lot more bad. With COVID-19, and so many clients out of work, and having to put off care for their pets...it sucked.

"Sit in on the Happy Hour with me," he urged. "We're starting in five minutes. The guys are a riot."

Lissa didn't understand Cade's obsession with metal. Oh, some of it wasn't too bad, some of the stoner metal or doom was fine, with the thick heavy bass behind all the guitars and drums. But the other subgenres? The growling, the shouting?

No thanks.

But she'd heard Cade talk about his metal friends over the past year. They got together at local shows, the ones that lived in the LA area. Other friends lived all over the country, and they only got to see each other at the bigger festivals like Maryland Death Festival or the Decibel Metal and Beer Festival or Northwest TerrorFest. They seemed like nice guys: a couple were musicians themselves, and several worked for music related publications, but there were other white-collar professionals, teachers and lawyers and doctors, as well as some blue collar guys. Even a couple women.

And now they'd started Friday night Heavy Metal Happy Hour, just to chat and get some human contact. Especially since all the upcoming festivals and concerts were cancelled.

Cade scootched the laptop so she could see the screen. He'd started up the Zoom app. So far it was just Cade and her, but two other people popped up while she was watching.

"Ryan! Mike!" Cade said. "Meet my baby sister Lissa."

"Hey." Lissa waved at the screen. God, she looked like death warmed over. Working at the clinic kept her on her feet and busy, so her figure was still trim, at least, but she missed going to the gym. And getting out in the sun.

"Dude, when are you going to get the green screen figured out? I'm tired of looking at your house," one of the two guys said. He had dark red hair and bright blue eyes, and was wearing a black t-shirt with an unreadable band name and some skeletal trees. He held up a fancy beer glass with curvy sides. "Cheers, Lissa. Nice to meet you from afar."

"Ryan's in Seattle," Cade said. "And I think it's my computer. It's too old. I'm on a buying moratorium right now though."

"Except for beer, right, dude?"

"Beer's essential. No worries about that."

"Hi, Lissa," the other guy, Mike, said. He was cute, *really* cute, with dark hair and green eyes and tanned cheekbones to die for.

"Hi. I guess you're Mike?"

"Yep. San Diego." He stretched, muscled arms flexing, tummy flat under his Slayer t-shirt.

Yum! Lissa perked up. San Diego wasn't that far.

Of course, in this time of the COVID-19 plague and essential travel only, he might as well be in New York.

More people popped up on the screen, each square getting disappointedly smaller. Nearly everyone was wearing some sort of black t-shirt. Band shirts, she guessed. She couldn't even read Mike's t-shirt any more.

The conversation really kicked in—everything from music to politics to new beers to what they were all binging on Netflix or even just reading (a lot of science fiction, apparently).

Lissa sat back and just listened. Looked like Mike, in his little square in the upper right of the screen, was content to do the same.

It was nice to hear voices other than Cade's and her co-workers, even when it was people she didn't know.

She always thought she was an introvert, but turned out she did crave some human contact.

Even if it was peripheral.

"I'm texting to see if Randy has any leftovers," she said to Cade as he laughed at someone's joke. Randy often did drop off food. He was a sweetheart that way. Lissa had initially hoped he and Cade would hook up, but then some other guy came into the picture and that was that.

Randy texted her back. *Bolognese and garlic bread. Got a plate just for you. And for Cade if he's the one to fetch it.*

Hmm. Maybe there was hope. Maybe that other guy didn't work out.

"Randy will feed you if you get it," she told Cade. Was that a flash of interest in her brother's eyes? "Oops—looks like someone messaged you."

Cade clicked to enlarge the chat window. It was a private message, not to the group.

And...oh! it was to her.

Cade smirked then pushed the laptop to her. "I'll go get dinner. Hey, everyone, I'll be right back, gotta go pick up dinner from our tenant."

Mike. The message was from Mike.

*Hi.*

Well, that wasn't much. *Hi back,* she typed.

*Cade talks about you all the time. That you're a vet. That's awesome.*

Oh, god, what was Cade telling his friends about her?

*Do you have any pets?* she asked. Oh, that was lame.

*A white and gray pit bull named Spike. After Spike from Buffy. He's a sweetheart, the gentlest dog I've ever met. And a black cat named Emma. She's in charge.*

*The cats usually are :)*

*LOL*

Gah, what to say? She'd never seen Buffy the Vampire Slayer.
She bet it was streaming somewhere. She'd binge it. All of it.

*What do you do, since you know what I do?* she typed.

*Ugh, was afraid you'd ask. Boring as hell. CPA. Working from home, now,* he typed back.

A CPA? She wished her CPA was that hot.

*At least it's work, right? I'm a little scared going in to the clinic, I have asthma, but I need to work. The cats need us. The clinic, I mean.*

*Thank you. Thank you for being there. I know if something happened with Spike or Emma I'd be desperate to get them help.*

Lissa squirmed. It was her job. She started typing "it's my job!" then deleted it. What are you supposed to say to something like that?

*Oops. Looks like things are winding down,* Mike typed. Lissa hadn't even noticed, had blocked out the conversation to focus on Mike. *Will you join the chat next week? On your own computer? :)*

*I guess. Sure.*

*Stay safe.*

*You too.* It was just the two of them left on the app. His square was big again. He had a sweet smile. Kind eyes. His nose was just the tiniest bit crooked. And he had the cutest dimple in his chin.

He waved at her, then his square disappeared.

She closed the app.

"HEY, LISSA!" Cade greeted her as she walked in the front door. Smelled like Korean short ribs. Randy was branching out.

"You're joining us for Happy Hour, right?" Cade continued.

"Gotta change!" Lissa said, dashing past him to the laundry room. Scrubs, mask, socks, into the washing machine. She kept her bra on (a real bra today, not a chest-flattening sports bra), and added a cute boho top, gauzy cotton embroidered with flowers along the neckline. And jeans. Cade wouldn't care if she wandered around in her underwear, but she wasn't going to go pantless. Even if it was a thing.

Bathroom next. Her makeup still looked good, her smoky eye shadow highlighting her gray eyes. She fluffed out her hair. Hopefully a bit more Liz Taylor than Morticia Adams this time.

She slid into the dining room chair. Cade had set up both of their laptops on the table, and poured each of them a beer. He'd saved the bottle to show the guys. Stone Ruination Double IPA.

He let her sit at the head of the table, opposite the window.

"Ooh, that's dressed up for you. And the lighting will be good for you," he said, then snickered.

"Going to get leftovers from Randy?" she said pointedly. They'd eaten well last week: the pasta bolognese; lasagna; and some delicious chard garlic sausage pasta. Cade had picked up the dinner each time, taking longer and longer each time to return.

Cade shut up.

She clicked to open the app on her laptop. Mike was already there, wearing a Ramones t-shirt this time. Cute. She liked punk, even if she didn't like metal.

Lissa clicked straight to private chat.

*Hi Mike.*

*Hi back,* he typed. *How was your week?*

*Ended up good,* she typed. *Busy, but things I could fix.*

*Me too. I helped some clients get small business loans set up. It'll keep their businesses going at least a couple more months. Felt good to be able to do something to help someone.*

*I watched* Buffy, she admitted. *Hadn't seen it before. I'm watching* Angel *now. I think I like it better so far.*

*I cosplayed Angel at ComiCon. I didn't have the guts to bleach my hair to be Spike.*

*Ooh, pics! I need pics! I went to ComiCon once. It was too crazy for me. Too many people.*

*There's quiet areas. You just have to know where. Maybe next year I can take you. Or the year after, if it's cancelled for both this and next year.*

Oh, crap. What should she say???

*Or not, if you don't want to.*

How could typing come across as disappointed? His square was little, a dozen people having joined the chat. But she could tell.

*No, that sounds great. I'd love to. I still want pics, though.*

*Here's my number if you want to text,* he typed. *Or maybe even talk. :)*

*Texting you now so you have my number.* She wondered if he could see how anxious she was.

*Great. Can I call you tomorrow?*

*Sure!*

~

SATURDAY AFTERNOON. Lissa had worked in the clinic that morning, getting a blocked tomcat catheterized so he could pee, in between all the other appointments. After the craziness of the clinic, she needed to get outside. Walk. Clear her head.

Cade was visiting Randy. Lissa wasn't sure what sort of social distancing was still in place, but it was the happiest she'd seen Cade in years. And god knew, Randy only left the house, wearing a mask and gloves, to go to Osteria Ripeteri to pick up groceries, since the restaurant turned the dining room into a pop up grocery store. He was good as family even if the two weren't an item.

*Busy?* Mike, texting.

*Just out for a walk. Wanna join me?* She loved her neighborhood, the hills, the eucalyptus and palms intermingled. The houses ranged from Craftsman to Spanish to Moderne like hers, then to 1950s ranches, 1990s Mediterranean, and now those boxy white pseudo Coastal things. Regardless, there was variety.

She'd love to share that with him. See if he felt the same.

Her phone rang. Mike, just him, on a video call.

"Hey, gorgeous," he said. His voice sounded deeper through the phone rather than the tinny computer speakers.

"Hi, you," she replied. She was in a tank and a bright pink patterned workout skort, and her hair was pulled up in a ponytail, but she didn't care how she looked. It was great just to talk, really talk, to Mike, just the two of them.

Well, and Mrs Martin from across the street, walking her Bichon Snowball, frowning at her. Mrs Martin wore a cloth mask. Lissa had skipped hers, trusting she could stay more than a dozen feet away from any fellow pedestrians.

"Where are you walking?"

She turned the phone around and scanned the neighborhood with it. "Just a couple blocks from my house."

"What a neat old neighborhood!" he said. "Mine is similar, including the hills and the mix of houses. It's a good workout just walking around."

That's how she felt. Exactly how she felt. "Where are you?"

"Just at home." He flipped his phone around, panned it around. "This is my living room."

It looked comfortable. A big dark brown leather couch layered with colorful Pendleton wool blankets, Spike at one end with Emma cuddled up against him. Oak floors like hers. White walls, and a tiled arched fireplace. A cozy leather armchair and a solid looking coffee table piled with books.

"Spanish bungalow?" she guessed.

"Spot on. 1928," he said. "Still got the original bathroom tiles."

"Awesome!"

"Pink and black."

"Even better."

"Aha. A pink bathroom lover."

"One of the few. One of the proud."

"Even if I have to remodel it one day I'm keeping the pink. It just adds character, you know?"

Lissa agreed. "We kept the original tiles in our duplex. Mint green downstairs, baby blue upstairs. And the original tubs. They're solid. Had to get new fixtures though."

"Even though things were made well, they only last so long," he said.

"Heading up the hill," Lissa said. "Excuse me if I pant."

"I'd love to hear that," he said. Then even through the phone, turned bright red. "Oops."

She giggled. Giggled! And chugged up the hill. An eight percent grade, it did take effort.

"When I want a really good workout, I speedwalk up and jog down and repeat," she said once she'd reached the top.

"I go to the beach and run in the sand."

"That sounds good. But I'm a good half hour plus away from the beach, even without traffic."

"Come visit me when all this crap is over," he said. "Let me take you to the beach."

"As long as you come visit me the next weekend up here, and I'll take you up into the Hollywood hills."

"Done."

"I'm serious."

"Me too. Dead serious," he said. "I really wish we'd met each other before all this crap."

She was quiet. "Me too," she said finally. "But we can keep doing this. Reaching out. Talking."

"Maybe catch some episodes of *Angel* together?" he said.

"Absolutely. Okay. *Star Trek* or *Star Wars*?"

"Both, sorry."

"That's okay. I'd say *Star Wars* but I really liked *Deep Space Nine*. And *Picard*."

"Haven't watched *Picard* yet. Let's see...Cade said you get pretty nerdy. *Shaun of the Dead* or *Slither*?"

"Can't choose. But dude! What about *Return of the Living Dead*?" She stuck her arms straight out. "Send...more...paramedics! And the half dog was perfect." The zombie gas had escaped within a medical teaching supply warehouse, including cadavers, pinned butterflies, and a preserved dog split longitudinally so its anatomy could be studied.

All of it, of course, re-animated.

"Eww. What about *Dawn of the Dead*. The first remake."

"Too dark for me," she said. "I like my zombies with a side of humor."

"*Fright Night?*"

"The original. Chris Sarandon was just dreamy."

"Well, the vamp in the sequel was pretty hot. The sister." He paused. "Looked a bit like you."

"Hmph," Lissa said, but she smiled. "I'm heading home. When do you want to talk next?"

"A movie tonight?" he asked. "If that's not too soon. Have you seen *Birds of Prey* yet?"

"Not yet—"

"I'll send you an Amazon gift card. Buy it and we'll sync watching it." Mike paused. "Is that okay?"

"Sounds great," Lissa said. And it did. It'd been ages since she'd been on a date, and god only knew, this would be the closest she was going to get in at least a couple months.

But damn it, she was going to enjoy it. And this all had to end sometime. And even if this was some weird blip, even if life wouldn't go back to the previous normal, she was going to live her life, the best she could.

"It's a date?"

She smiled. "It's a date."

# A SIP TO HER HEART

*L*illian swiped the smooth sanded surface of the reclaimed wood bar top one last time, not missing a single inch of the warm gray wood. The cloth snagged on her work-roughened hands.

She had some unscented lotion she could use. Didn't want to compete with the wine. No perfume, no scented lotion.

It was Lillian's first day on the job at J. Bast, pouring single-vineyard Zinfandels and Cabs from the hills on the eastern edge of Napa Valley. She'd been here many times as a guest, but never on the working side of the bar top.

The J. Bast tasting room would open in five minutes, 11:00 a.m. sharp.

She put a record, Roxy Music *Avalon*, on the turntable, and the soft mellow tones filled the tasting room. Sure, it took time to flip the records over, to take them out of their album sleeves and put them back in, but at J. Bast, you weren't supposed to be in a rush. Just sit back, sip the wine, soak in the ambience.

The tasting room itself was in an old storefront on an oak-lined side street off Highway 29 in St Helena, with exposed red brick walls dating from 1921 and a polished stained-concrete floor. Besides the bar top, with its leather and steel stools, vintage faded red kilim rugs anchored two different seating areas, defined by low, blocky, reclaimed-wood coffee tables and plush pine green velvet sectionals that Lillian had sunk into many an afternoon.

The tasting room smelled of wine-stained oak barrels and minerally brick, and you could anticipate the richness and complexity of the wine just by standing still and breathing in.

J. Bast was just a short walk from her mid-renovations 1920s bungalow. Bonus! *And* she could bring Barret, her English Cocker Spaniel, to work with her. Even better. Winery dogs were a thing; there was even a book about them, with photos of each dog and a blurb about his or her winery.

Barret had come wine tasting with Lillian to a variety of dog-friendly wineries and tasting rooms throughout the valley over the past summer and fall, greeting every new person he met with the surety that person would love him, his stubby tail wagging furiously and his eyes like melted chocolate.

Right now he was lounging upside down on his favorite dog bed, cream fleece lining and preppy navy and cream mattress ticking outer fabric. She'd tucked the bed halfway under the bar top, next to a box of new Spiegelau glasses. Barret was chewing on his favorite stuffed mallard drake toy with his eyes closed, twitching one back paw.

If he squeezed the duck just right, it would quack. Loudly.

Luckily he usually focused on the head and wings, rather than the body with the quacker.

As good as company as Barret was, and as hard as she was working on her house, she'd been going stir crazy the past few months.

Going from burned out swing shift ER doc to early retirement had sounded great.

And initially, it was. When she wasn't out exploring Napa valley, Lillian focused on her house, all by herself for most of the grunt work, hiring out the electrical and plumbing. She was good with her hands. Careful. Methodic. She stripped all the woodwork of decades of layers of paint. Refinished the narrow-planked oak floors. Attacked the kitchen first, then the bathrooms. Took first the powder room down to the studs and renovated it with vintage inspired blue wall tiles and black and white hex floor tiles, then did the same to the full bath (switching to jade green and black and white).

She didn't consider herself an extrovert. But she did need *some* human interaction, after months of work, most of it solitary, on the house. And she could turn on peppiness when dealing with the public. And she loved, loved, loved, wine.

Hence the part-time job at J. Bast. The same dedication she'd had towards being a doctor, then learning how to fix up her house, she was going to apply to learning about wine.

Oh, she'd drank wine for years. Decades. And knew a fair amount, as a foodie into wine pairing and tasting menus. But she wasn't a sommelier, and that's the knowledge she craved.

Lillian pulled up the schedule on the computer. She was working til 3 p.m., just a four hour shift. Tastings were scheduled on the hour, though they often lasted longer, and today was fully booked. Jackie Bast herself would be in around 2:30 p.m., and staying til the tasting room closed three hours later.

Lillian was thinking she might take a quick lunch break then come back to J. Bast. Soak in some wine knowledge, just listening to Jackie with the power-buying clients. Cleaning glasses. Making herself useful.

She'd put some short ribs in the slow cooker, so she wouldn't have to prepare much for her dinner, later. She had time, plenty of time.

Lillian pulled out the bottles for today's tasting from the wine fridges. A rosé from the cooler fridge, and the everyday Zin (as Lillian thought of it), three single vineyard Zins, and a Cab from the red wine fridge. She uncorked all the bottles (well, the rosé was a screwtop, it could wait) and decanted the Cab. Lined up two sets of glasses with their delicate stems on the bar top. A smaller white wine glass for the rosé, and five of the larger Spiegelau red wine glasses, for each of the clients. She grabbed a single red wine glass for herself.

11:05. Where were the clients for the 11:00 a.m.?

Rude to be late. Especially since J. Bast was likely the first wine tasting stop of the day for them.

"Maybe I'm not cut out for this job," Lillian said to Barret. He blinked up at her, wagged his tail, then *quacked* the duck.

She opened the rosé and poured herself a tiny taste. Oh, yum. Strawberry and rose petals but not at all sweet; crisp and refreshing. Provence-style. J. Bast didn't have a lot of this rosé left, just a half dozen cases. Lillian was surprised it hadn't sold out over the summer. She herself had bought a couple cases. Even if it was gray, cold, and rainy, she could still picture drinking a glass, curled up on the couch with a chicken salad sandwich for lunch.

11:10. Lillian poured herself some of the everyday Zin. She *did* have to taste each bottle. Make sure nothing was corked or otherwise off. Everyday Zin. Stonefruit, cherry mostly, but not a jam bomb. At $35 per bottle, it was the guilt-free red of the bunch. She had a couple bottles at home.

She wiped off the bar top again. Polished off the stainless steel dump buckets. Arranged the sets of glasses in arcs rather than a straight line on the bar top in front of the two stools.

11:20.

Okay, she took this job to be social. Meet people. (*Maybe even meet a man,* her reptile brain interjected.) Share the excitement about wine.

And all she was doing was standing here.

She poured herself some of the next Zin. Benny's Vineyard, named after Jackie's dad. The vines were all at least fifty years old, clinging to the side of the mountain. Tenacious. Tough. Amazing that the wine could be so nuanced and subtle. Plum and minerals. It cried out for meat, but nothing too heavy. Maybe a dried cherry-stuffed pork loin. Or maybe some gorgonzola and figs.

Maybe she could brainstorm a cheese plate to pair with the wines.

Damn, now she was hungry *and* annoyed.

11:40. She put *I Can Feel the Heat Beating as One* on turntable. Yo La Tengo, her favorite band. Alt indie.

She'd tasted all the wines. She was sipping a half glass of rosé, rearranging the napkins on one of the coffee tables, when a man finally entered the tasting room.

A man. Singular. The tasting was supposed to be for two people.

His short cut graying brown hair was tousled. It looked soft, and Lillian had the urge to run her fingers through it.

She would swear one sock was navy blue, the other hunter green. Neither dark color looked great with the pale tan suede of his driving moccasins. But above his ankles? He wore faded jeans that were molded to muscular thighs and a white button-down shirt with the sleeves rolled up to expose equally defined forearms. His face was boyish, with faint crow's feet and laugh lines aging him to early-mid fifties. Her age.

Cute, she supposed, but *late*. But cute.

*Really* cute, despite her annoyance.

"Welcome to J. Bast," Lillian said. "Are you my eleven o'clock, finally?"

She winced. Hoped that didn't sound as bitchy as she feared.

But she bet it did.

DAMNIT. Jeff hadn't meant to be late. He was *never* late.

But then his friend old college friend Bruce had gotten a call from Bruce's ex Tom, and Tom being Tom and Bruce being Bruce, Bruce had to pack up and have Jeff drop him off for the airport shuttle, cutting short their yearly wine country trip.

But they'd missed the 10 a.m. shuttle, so Jeff had driven him all the way to Vallejo to pick it up there. At that point it was a toss-up on whether he should just drop off Bruce at SFO, but Jeff *really* didn't want to miss this tasting.

He'd read up on J. Bast and their focus on Zins, and he was ready for something other than the (albeit delicious) Cabs he'd been tasting all week. More than ready.

And now he was 40 minutes into his tasting, without having tasted a drop of wine.

But damn....that woman looked good. What did you call them? Wine baristas? Most of the places had dewy-eyed blonde twenty-somethings manning the bar tops, but this woman was closer to his age. Mid forties to his fifty-two, maybe. Her green eyes, fringed by thick dark lashes, were bright against her lightly tanned face. Her slim nose was just a little crooked, like she'd broken it and not worried about getting it straightened.

She wore tight dark blue jeans, tucked into low black cowboy boots. The jeans showcased her rangy curves, as did the sleeveless turtle necked black sweater. A stylized, angular, black dog tattoo decorated the muscular deltoid of her right arm.

She had sun-streaked brown hair pinned up in a messy bun at the nape of her neck.

He wanted to unpin it. Run his fingers through it.

Say he was sorry for making her mad.

Because she looked plenty pissed.

"Are you my eleven o'clock, finally?" she asked. Her voice was rough, sending shivers down his back, like a cat's tongue licking his hand.

"I am," he said. "Jeff Danvers. I'm sorry I'm so late. I had to drop off my friend Bruce at the airport shuttle, and we missed it, so I had to go to Vallejo—"

"Well, you're here now. I take it Bruce was also going to be tasting?"

Jeff nodded. "I'll pay for his tasting still." He didn't know how the wine baristas got paid, but if it was on commission, he didn't want her to bear the brunt of Bruce's hasty exit.

He'd have to buy extra wine to make up for Bruce, too.

"Not necessary," she said. "I'm Lillian. Is this your first time at J. Bast?"

He nodded. "Yes, and I'm really exci—"

The phone rang. "Let me get that," Lillian said as she headed back to the bar top and snagged the phone. "J. Bast—oh, you're calling to cancel? Thanks for letting me know, and I'm sorry you won't be making it today. Would you like to reschedule? Oh, okay, just call us anytime, thanks."

She turned to face Jeff. "You're in luck. The noon canceled. That was them, calling to let me know."

"I'm so sorry I didn't call to say I was running late. I just wanted to get here as fast as I could." He smiled winsomely as he sat on one of the leather and steel barstools. Thin-stemmed wine glasses were arranged in a precise arc in front of him, gleaming against the soft gray wood of the bar top. Nice.

His smile usually got him out of trouble.

Not this time, it looked like, as she poured him a taste of rosé. "2019 Rosé. It's a blend of Grenache, Cinsault, and a few other varietals. The grapes are sourced from the Dry Creek Valley in Sonoma."

Was she always this grouchy?

And why did he want to make *her* smile? It had been years since he'd met a woman who attracted him like this one did.

"Pour yourself some?" he said.

She gestured with her glass, a quarter full with pale peachy pink wine.

"Oh. Um, pour yourself a bit more?"

There it was. Just a bit of a smirk on her face.

*QUACK!*

"Oh gosh. I'm sorry, that's my dog—"

"Your dog quacks like a duck?"

"His toy does." She disappeared behind the counter, reappearing with a moist tattered green and brown plush duck toy.

"See?" she said, squeezing it. It quacked. She tossed it onto one of the kilim rugs and a medium sized black and white dog tore around the counter after it.

"Oh, you have an English Cocker?" Jeff asked, delighted. His aunt back in New York bred and showed English Cockers. They were wonderful dogs, always happy. Jeff hopped off the barstool and sat on the rug next to the dog. "Oh, he's handsome. What's his name?"

"Barret," Lillian said. Disloyal creature, he was half in Jeff's lap already, ready for belly rubs.

"That's great you get to bring him to work."

"Well, it depends on how it goes. This is my first day."

"And your first client shows up late, and your next cancels. I'm sorry."

She smiled. Score!

"You don't have to keep apologizing," she said. "I'm a bit of a perfectionist, and I like to have things just so. I let it get to me, and I shouldn't have."

"Well, not to mess up your routine again, but can we do the tasting over here on the floor? That way I can play with your dog and drink wine."

Lillian laughed, a deep throaty chuckle that outdid her voice.

"I don't think he's going to let you up." She carefully arranged the glasses on the nearest coffee table, then fetched the bottles. "Did you like the rosé?"

"Loved it. Summer in a glass."

"Great! That's what I think too. Next up is what I call the everyday Zin. It's really nice, but not too expensive. If you're grilling burgers, this is what you'd crack open." She poured a healthy amount of wine in his glass.

"Gah, don't talk food. I had to skip breakfast to get Bruce to the shuttle."

"Oh no. We don't have any food here. I was just thinking earlier we should do some cheese plates or something. We can get delivery from Gott's, if a burger sounds good. They also have an ahi sandwich."

"A burger sounds great. I can order online?"

"Yep—"

He pulled out his cell phone, swiped and typed.

"Two burgers and fries, coming up," he said a few minutes and sips of wine later.

"Oh, you didn't have to get me anything—"

"Of course I did. I wouldn't eat in front of you without sharing, and I wanted my own burger." He grinned. "Does this make this our first date?"

*FIRST DATE?*

Lillian hadn't been on a date in years. Not since that carpenter from Oakland, when she was restoring her Victorian in San Francisco. And that wasn't really a date. Just some sweaty victory sex after struggling all day to install some kitchen cabinets.

"First date?" she squeaked. "I thought you were from out of town."

"San Jose. Is that too far?"

"It's too fast." Her lower back tensed and a pain shot down her left leg. *Breathe. Relax.* Gah, this always happened when she got stressed. She retired to get away from stress. Not to add more. She tensed her toes, then relaxed them. Then her calves, her quads, her glutes.

By the time she got to her pecs she was okay. Well, better. Functional.

"Okay, it's our first Zin and burgers," he said. "No pressure. Doesn't even have to be a future second Zin and burgers."

"I can handle that," Lillian said. "I mean, Zin and burgers. That sounds okay."

"And I know where to find you. In a non-stalker way," he added hastily as she tensed up again.

He grabbed the duck and quacked it, then tossed it for Barret to chase.

"My dog likes you," she said.

"That means I'm a good guy, right?"

"He likes everyone."

"Well, that's English Cockers for you. Do I get brownie points for knowing the breed at least?"

"A couple."

"And I really like this Zin," he continued.

"A couple more points." She smiled tentatively. He did seem nice. And he was cute. And he was trying pretty darn hard.

"What's the next wine? Will it go with burgers too?"

"I think you can drink any Zin with burgers," she said. "But I'd probably pair this one with the ahi. Benny's Vineyard, single vineyard old vines. You can taste the hillside in this one. The minerals, the vines fighting to produce their fruit." She poured them both a generous taste.

"You really love wine, don't you?" he said.

She nodded. "That all that flavor can be pulled out of something as simple as a grape? The potential of it all. And it tastes so good. It's why I retired here."

"Ah. So wine barista is not your first career?"

"Wine barista? That's cute." she said. "But no. ER doc. Until I got too burned out. Had to get away from it all. I need something relaxing, but I hate to say, I think I make whatever I do stressful. What about you?"

"I've sold a couple start-ups. Thinking of getting a house somewhere in the valley, so I can drink more wine." He grinned.

"St Helena's really nice."

"Yeah, I'm renting an Airbnb here. An old Victorian. Really neat house."

"You like old houses?"

"Love them."

What had she been thinking earlier? Maybe meet a man?

She might be a perfectionist. She might expect way too much out of herself.

But one thing she wasn't: a coward.

And so she heard herself say, "Short ribs. Short ribs would go great with this wine.

"And I have a great old house you should check out. If you like old houses. 7 p.m. work for you?"

She met his eyes squarely. And met his grin with one of her own.

Barret chomped on his duck.

QUACK!

# THE CATS OF HIS HEART

*J*oe was just waiting his turn at the four way stop sign, swigging some lukewarm coffee from his steel travel mug.

Ah, the taste of ocean water and black coffee in the morning!

Hermosa Beach hometown heroes Black Flag blared from his speakers. He was on his way home from an awesome surfing set at El Porto, snuggled up in a Stanford hoodie and a pair of camo cargo shorts against the late fall morning chill, ready to tackle the work day.

—when the guy in the black Tesla SUV barreled through the intersection.

Joe clenched his steering wheel. He saw it, he knew the Tesla guy didn't, cell phone up to his ear, and he, Joe, just didn't have time to do anything—

—saw the tiny orange kitten, scared by who knows what, a dog on the wood chip path with its tall eucalyptus trees, between the two parallel streets at this wonky intersection, who cares about that, the kitten *darted into the street*—

And the Tesla hit it. Didn't even slow down.

Joe registered the woman on the bicycle, at the stop sign on the other side of the street, who stood up on her pedals, muscular legs powering her road bike, chasing after the Tesla.

Heard her bellow, a lioness's roar coming out of her diminutive frame, "ASSHOLE!" and saw her slam her fist on the trunk of the Tesla as it gunned off, before she gave up and unclipped her shoes from her pedals, heedless of her bike toppling to the road, and ran to the still little body.

He didn't even realize he was standing there with her, til he said, "You can put your bike in the back of my pickup. I'll get us to a vet clinic."

She yanked off her bike jersey, exposing a faded black sports bra and a trim stomach, and gently placed the little kitten onto the red and yellow bike jersey, using it as an impromptu sling, trying to keep the kitten as still as possible. He grabbed her bike (carbon fiber, *nice*) off the street and placed it into his pick up bed on top of his longboard, then opened up the passenger door for her to slide in.

" He's still breathing. There's a clinic on Pacific Coast Highway and 6th," the woman said. Her voice was rich, husky, sent shivers down his spine. Like drinking old Scotch. In front of the fireplace, up in the mountains, at night, during a snowstorm.

She gently, tentatively, stroked the kitten. The kitten moved its head, opened its eyes, made that squeaky high pitched mew kittens did.

"Gotcha. I know it." He drove to it quickly but carefully, continuing on the street paralleling the wood chip path until 5th, turning left onto PCH then a right onto 6th and a quick right into the parking lot. It all took longer than he wanted even though it was only a few miles.

He let her hop out of the pickup with the kitten and run inside before he parked.

He parked and started to head in, thought twice, and grabbed her bike and wheeled it in with him.

Last thing that woman needed was for her bike to get stolen.

The clinic itself smelled clean, a memory of bleach and lavender air freshener, but there was a very doggy-smelling hound to the right.

A fluffy frou frou dog lifted its leg on the plant to the left of the doorway as he watched, adding the pungent smell of urine to the mix. Padded benches sat on other side of the doorway. A semi-circular receptionist counter was directly in front of him. On the far right of the counter a coffee machine percolated. A jar of cookies (labeled *For Humans*) sat next to it.

The woman was at the receptionist counter. The kitten wasn't with her.

A female technician, dressed in navy blue scrub bottoms and a colorful scrub top patterned with kittens and balls of yarn, came out from the back area, and handed the woman's bike jersey to her.

"She's doing fine," the tech said softly, touching the woman's arm. "We've got an IV catheter going with some fluids, some pain meds, and we're getting some x rays now."

"Thanks," the woman said, her straight rigid back relaxing, her husky voice soft.

"Can you fill out this paperwork? It's your kitten, right?" The receptionist, a slim Latinx woman, handed a clipboard to the woman.

"She's a stray, I just saw this total asshole hit her." Her face fell. "I can't have pets at my apartment. I'll pay for her care, I said I would, but I can't keep her."

"Well, we'll scan her for a microchip, and if she is chipped, we'll contact the company to see if she's registered," the receptionist said. "If there's no chip, I can give you a list of rescues if you'd like, to see if one can take her."

"I can keep her," Joe said, stepping up next to the woman.

"And you are?" asked the receptionist doubtfully.

"Joe. Joe Alvarez. I saw it all happen, too." He took the brown, old-school clipboard and started filling out the paperwork. He wasn't going to think about this, he was just going to do it, darn it.

Wasn't going to think about Lucy.

The woman sniffed her bike jersey, then folded it up, clenched it one hand.

"I think she peed on it," she said. She held out her other hand to

Joe. "Charlie Arden. Thanks for giving me a ride. And bringing my bike in."

She smiled, a hearty smile that spoke of guffaws and beers after bike rides and sheer fun. A smile that went with that rich voice. Both the smile and the voice were bigger than her.

That was it. He'd thought she was a badass before, chasing the Tesla, but that smile undid him. That, and her muscular curves packed into that tiny frame, apparent in her sports bra and black bike shorts. Her curly brunette hair was up in a long ponytail, hair he'd love to run his fingers through. Her warm gold green eyes just added to the appeal. She had a strong face, rather than a pretty one, with broad freckled cheekbones and a firm chin.

She clacked over to the brown vinyl covered, padded bench against the wall, plopped down, and pulled off her bike shoes. "Doubt they want me scuffing up their floor," she said matter-of-factly, stretching out her sock-clad feet.

He grabbed a couple cookies (chocolate chip, his favorite!) from the *For Humans* cookie jar and two cups of coffee, then sat next to her. "That was really brave of you," he said, handing her a cookie and a cup of coffee.

She shrugged. "Anyone would've done the same."

He chewed on the cookie, the sweetness of the cookie mixed with the dark chocolate chips hitting the post-surfing spot, and thought of all the other cars at the intersection. He and Charlie were the only people to check on the kitten. Of course, maybe other people thought they had it all handled, but...

"Do you really want to keep her?" Charlie asked.

Joe considered. "I do."

"You sound not quite sure."

"It's a big responsibility," he said. "But I've missed having a cat. The best ones find you, you know?

"And I'll pay for her care, don't worry," he added.

That firm chin of hers stuck out.

"I said I would," she said.

And didn't say a word after that.

Hᴏᴡ ᴅᴀʀᴇ he insinuate she couldn't pay. Yeah, things were a little tough right now, but she said she would. And she would, even if she had to max out her credit card.

She wished she could keep the kitten herself.

She'd been lonely since the divorce. Her ex George had brought his border collie Maggie to their relationship, and left with her as well, even though Charlie had spent more time with that sweet dog than George ever bothered.

Honestly, she missed Maggie more than George.

George was an asshole, like the guy in the Tesla. Too much money, thinking too much of himself. Good riddance.

Easy to think that in the light of day, when she kept herself busy. Evenings were harder.

This guy, Joe, seemed alright. Soft brown eyes, dark hair flopping over like he was a mid thirties escapee from a boy band, that long lanky build. He stopped for the kitten and brought her bike in. Thoughtful.

"You kick ass," he said, breaking the silence, looking up from filling in the form on the clipboard.

She glanced at him. He had a sweet grin. He was leaning back against the bench, long legs stretched out in front of him, tanned feet in leather flip flops.

"I can take care of myself," she said.

"Don't doubt it for a minute. Hey, I expect they'll be keeping her for the day to make sure she's okay. Want to grab some coffee? Some real coffee? I have a couple meetings today, but they're in the after-noon." He looked shy, all of a sudden. If he chewed on his lower lip she'd start giggling.

She had the time. She didn't have any work for today. That was part of the problem. Initially she'd planned on biking all the way to Santa Monica and back. She'd gotten her bike, a nice carbon fiber road bike, fast and sleek, when she was married, when her voice over work was the icing on the cake to George's salary as a screenwriter for several popular Netflix series.

Then she'd found out he'd been cheating on her with a string of cheap Hollywood hookers.

She'd been humiliated. She had to get checked for STDs. Not that she and George had been doing much, the last year of their marriage.

Her body was fine, but her heart wasn't.

"Real coffee sounds good," she said. "But I don't have any other shoes." She hefted her biking shoes, showing the plastic cleats on the bottom. "Sucks to do anything in these except ride."

"I can take you home and you can change," he offered.

She looked at him suspiciously. "I can ride home and just get a spare pair of shoes and ride back."

"If that's what you'd rather do," he said. "Let me get this turned in, and find out what's up with the kitten."

TURNED out the kitten was just battered and bruised. No broken bones on the x-rays, and a quick lab test showed all her organ functions were normal for a kitten. The doctor still wanted to keep the kitten there for the day for observation and care.

"Lucky little thing," the doctor had commented, her blue eyes warm with concern. "And lucky you two found her."

"She can go home tonight?" Joe asked. He'd have to get all the stuff for a kitten. Litterbox, litter, toys, food, bowls... he didn't have anything left from Lucy. He couldn't bear to keep her things, after.

"Should be able to, as long as someone keeps an eye on her. We close at 6, so come by 5:30 or so to pick her up."

Joe already knew where the kitten would sleep. Right next to his pillow, curled up in a sleepy little ball of fluff. He'd keep an eye on her.

Charlie insisted on riding home.

"Where did you want to go?" she asked before clipping into her pedals. "I'll just meet you there."

"We can just do Starbucks, if you want. But there's a little local place in Riviera Village we can grab coffee then gelato next door if you'd rather do that."

"That sounds good," she said. "I haven't had gelato for awhile. I'll meet you in an hour or so." She pedaled off, bike jersey back on.

Joe figured it was going to be harder to get her to trust him, than the kitten.

CHARLIE CHECKED her messages soon as she got home, even before her quick shower.

Nothing. Nada. Nix.

She'd check her email next.

Nothing there, either. No job offers or inquiries. She emailed her agent, her weekly check in, just to keep her name in front of him.

Unless her emails were automatically filed. Then even that email wasn't doing any good.

She really needed some steady work.

California property laws being as they were, and with no pre-nup, she got half in the divorce. But she didn't want a thing George had touched. They'd sold their house in Manhattan Beach, split the accounts, but she socked everything away. Too practical to donate it all, she wanted the money out of sight.

Which meant she needed to earn her own keep. And not touch even the interest on that money. Which meant she watched her budget and lived in this tiny 1940s eight-plex, with out-of-code louvered windows and stained oak floors, that wouldn't even allow a kitten. *A kitten.*

She showered and tossed on a pair of faded tattered blue jeans that hugged her curves like a wetsuit. Snug black t-shirt. Doc Martens so she could stomp around if she wanted. Some days were stomping days. Today could be one of those.

Fluffed her hair from the ponytail, added a bit of mascara, that was it. He'd seen her in worse, all sweaty from biking.

She parked her aging Prius in the big parking lot near the coffee shop, fed the meter for two hours, then walked to the coffee shop.

Riviera Village, a cute commercial area in Redondo Beach, close to what was called the Riviera section of Torrance at the south end of the Santa Monica Bay, was jam-packed with trendy clothing stores, brew-pubs, and a mix of moderately pricy restaurants. It wasn't a crazy expensive scene like downtown Manhattan Beach, or even Hermosa Beach, and was a bit more family friendly.

Her stomach grumbled at the rich coffee smell, mixed with the sweeter smells of warmed up pastries, croissants and cookies and scones, as she went in. She hadn't eaten breakfast before her bike ride, and except for the cookie at the vet clinic, hadn't eaten anything yet today.

The coffee house was full of people with laptops, drinking coffee, tapping away at their keyboards, a happy buzz of work and conversation. She spotted Joe, sitting on a worn butterscotch leather couch, long legs crossed in front of him. He was reading a book: the most recent King novel? She couldn't read the title. He had a chipped turquoise coffee mug on the marble-topped side table next to the couch.

He hadn't seen her yet, so she went to order coffee and a snack. A ham and cheese croissant. She could count that as a snack and part of lunch. Drip coffee, with room for cream.

She plopped onto a cozy chintz armchair opposite the couch.

"Hi there," Joe said, closing his book, using a clean napkin as a bookmark.

"Whatcha reading?"

"King's newest. It's good."

Score one for her. She nibbled on her croissant. It was good, especially after her bike ride. Just the right amount of buttery flakiness with salty ham and tart cheese.

"So, what were you planning today, BK?" he asked.

"BK?"

"Before kitten," he said, smiling that sweet goofy grin.

"A longer bike ride," she said. "Then I don't know what. Send out resumes. Harass my agent."

"Agent?" he asked, leaning forward. "Are you an actress?"

"Voice," she admitted.

"Really. Wow. I mean, that's awesome. Cartoons, or?"

"Anything I can get, from commercials to audio books."

"Gaming?" he asked, his soft brown eyes suddenly sharp.

"Haven't done that," she said. "Why?"

"BK, I was just heading home to work. But this afternoon, I have a couple meetings, including one with a friend I went to school with about an app for gamers."

"Dude, are you one of those Silicon Valley tech bros?"

"Dude, do I look like one?" he asked sharply. "I grew up in East LA."

She glanced at his sweatshirt. "And went to school at Stanford."

He shrugged. "I worked hard. And had my mom and my teachers looking out for me."

"But you work on apps. Tech stuff." It was too much. It was too close to the culture George had been immersed in. Cutthroat, based on who knew who, misogynistic ... she couldn't deal with that again.

She wrapped up her croissant in a napkin, drank her coffee in one gulp. Some dribbled down her chin. She didn't care. "I gotta go."

WHAT DID HE SAY? He watched her stomp off, bumping into couches and chairs and people, barely stopping to say she was sorry.

Damn it. He liked her, and he got the feeling she liked him too. He'd had too many recent hook ups where the woman just seemed interested in his money. This one seemed to like him because of *him*.

Because he was the kind of guy to stop for a hurt kitten.

And he liked her, because she was the type of woman who was brave enough to chase down a car on just a bicycle.

And that husky, rich voice of hers. It would be perfect for his friend's app. It sounded like she needed work. It would be perfect.

He'd help his friend out, and he'd be able to help Charlie out. And have an excuse to see her more.

He called his friend. He was hoping, hoping with all his fingers and toes crossed, that he'd see Charlie one more time today. There was a chance, a tiny chance, that he would ....

"Hey, Rick? Can we schedule that meeting for 6:30 instead? Grab some dinner after?"

~

SHE WAS HALFWAY to her car before she could think straight.

Joe wasn't George. Not at all. George would never have stopped for a hurt *person*, let alone a kitten. Joe had worked hard for his apparent success. George got started because of his dad, and who his dad knew. Joe had a sweet goofy smile. George, handsome as he'd been, always had that cold look on his face.

They were both men. That was the only commonality.

And she'd blown it.

By the time she yanked open her car door, cringing at the scraping noise the door always made, and got in, she was ready to clutch the steering wheel, put her head down, and cry.

But she didn't.

She drove home, head up, and figured she'd chalk it up to one more lesson she'd learned in a long string of hard lessons.

This time, though, it was a lesson to maybe, just maybe, trust a little.

~

JOE SHOWED up to the clinic at 5:30 on the dot. He'd called earlier for an update, and the vet let him know the kitten was resting, but had eaten a full meal, and pooped, and peed, all of which was important. She was breathing fine, too, another concern allayed.

The tech, the same woman as earlier, but in a scrub top with puppies and bowls of kibble, gestured to him to go into one of the exam rooms. As he entered, he looked over his shoulder.

And there she was. Charlie, looking both stubborn and a little lost, wallet clutched in her hand, just coming through the front door.

"Charlie!" he called. "Charlie, come here, they're getting her for us to take home!"

"Us?" she said as she joined him in the exam room, her voice husky and sweet. Agave syrup in a mezcal margarita. She plopped into one of the two chairs in the room, opposite the exam table.

He blushed and sat next to her. "I was hoping you'd come to see her."

"I said I'd pay for her treatment—"

He placed his hand on hers, just for a moment. "I know," he said. "But that's not why I wanted you to show up."

The vet came in, cuddling the kitten against her chest. "She's such a little purr monster," she said, placing the kitten on the faded but clean towel on the exam table. "She did great. Cats are amazingly resilient creatures."

Joe had already jumped up, cooing at the kitten. His kitten. He shot a quick look at Charlie. *Their* kitten, if he was lucky. He kissed the top of her perfect fuzzy orange head.

THE VET CHUCKLED. "OKAY," she said, directing her words at Charlie. "You're obviously the practical one. Keep an eye out for any difficulty breathing. You see that, get her to the ER ASAP. Here's the info for the emergency clinic—" she passed Charlie a brochure, then a bag of hand-outs, a sample of food, and little baggies of treats—"and here's a kitten pack. She's old enough to start her shots, I think about 8 or 9 weeks, but we'll do a recheck next week and if she's okay, we'll start then. No microchip, so she's yours, unless you see any signs up for a lost kitten."

Charlie nodded. "Got it," she said.

"Any questions?" the vet asked.

"I don't think so," Charlie said. "Joe?"

He looked up from nuzzling the kitten, now cradled in his arms and purring madly, making biscuits with her white paws.

"Let's get her home," he said.

JOE COULDN'T BELIEVE IT. Well, he could; he figured luck was what you made it, and he'd figured she'd be back to the clinic to pay for the kitten's treatment. And he figured he could take advantage of the situation, get her to give him another chance.

He didn't argue with her about it as she paid, even though he saw her knuckles whiten when she clenched the pen to sign the credit card receipt.

"Do you want to see her new home?" he asked. "My house is just up on 3rd near Prospect. Little Spanish bungalow with a standalone office in the backyard. Perfectly safe for droids. And kittens." And women, his warm brown eyes implied.

She eyed him, evaluated, smirked at the droids comment. "Okay," she said.

And now she was on the couch in his office, playing with the kitten while they waited for Rick to show up. He'd told her about the project, watching her posture straighten the more he said.

"It does sound interesting," she said.

"Yoo hoo!" someone called from outside. "Joe, you there?"

A woman's voice.

"That's Rick?" Charlie asked, holding the kitten as Joe opened the door.

"Come on in, gorgeous!" he said, grabbing Rick and spinning her around in a huge hug.

"Charlie, meet Rick, Ricki, my best friend from college," Joe said, once done with properly greeting Rick. "Rick, this is the woman I was telling you about."

Rick, a tall curvy woman with wild dreadlocks and deep walnut colored skin, smiled at her. "Say something, darlin'," she said.

"Um…" Charlie was never, ever at a loss for words. Until now.

"Um…." Rick echoed, quirking an eyebrow.

"The kitten is adorable?"

"Well, she needs a script," Rick said, turning back to Joe, "but yeah, she's perfect."

"Don't I get a say in this?" Charlie asked.

"Course you do. But I do hope it's a yes." Rick smiled lazily at Joe. "She's just your type, isn't she? Your real type, not like all those other girls—"

"Rick!"

She smirked, then turned back to Charlie. "In all seriousness, you sound great. I'd love to take you both out to dinner so we can talk about the project."

RICK DROVE them to a restaurant just down the street. Joe had made reservations earlier. Charlie assumed that worst case, had she not shown up, just he and Rick would've eaten there.

After that, Rick drove back to her hotel. "We'll talk tomorrow," she said. "Sure you want to walk up the hill?"

Both Joe and Charlie nodded. She felt stuffed, and a walk, uphill or not, would be welcome.

Joe reached out for her hand halfway up the first hill. He shortened his long stride to match hers. "I hope you don't think I was presumptuous," he said. "It's just that you are a voice actor, and we needed one with your voice."

"And I needed a job," she said.

He shrugged. "Didn't matter. I wanted you regardless. You're perfect. For the job." He blushed.

She smirked and took his hand.

When they reached her car, he hesitated. "Would you like to come in?" he asked. "To the house, not just the office. I do want you to see where the kitten will live."

"Okay," she said after a moment. "You know, we keep calling her 'the kitten'. What are you going to name her?"

"Gelato?" he said, as he opened the front door, a heavy mahogany door with a decorative iron-barred window and a grilled speakeasy. He gestured to let her pass.

Charlie looked around the living room. It smelled like vanilla candles, but not overwhelming. A cozy slip-covered sofa sat against one wall. The opposite wall looked out to the front, and was filled by a gorgeous rectangular window, panes of old wavy glass. To the right an arched entrance led to the dining room.

To the left was a fireplace, with original turquoise, red, and cobalt blue deco tiles. And above it was a framed watercolor of a dainty orange cat lounging on the slipcovered sofa, her green eyes imperious.

"Oh," Charlie said. "Who is that?"

"That was Lucy," Joe said. "My cat through high school, and college, and up to just a couple years ago. She died of lymphoma when she was seventeen."

"I'm so sorry," she said.

"You know how some pets are just special? I mean they all are, but—"

"She was the cat of your heart," Charlie said, her rich voice soft.

"Yes." She understood. Joe's heart swelled.

They stood quietly together for a moment. "Okay," he said. "But the kitten. I left her in the bathroom, just in case, well, just in case." He went through the dining room to the hallway beyond, and opened the middle door.

The kitten crept out, eyes wide, tail fluffed.

"Oh, you poor baby," crooned Charlie, picking her up, cuddling her, breathing in her fur, then passing her to Joe.

He held her against his chest, feeling her little body relax against his.

"Tess," Charlie said. "What about Tess?"

"That fits. That does," Joe said. He stroked the kitten's—Tess's!—

back. "Um, can I see you again? I mean, I know we're having another meeting tomorrow with Rick, but I mean after. Like dinner. Or drinks."

"Or just hanging out here with your kitten?" Charlie asked.

"Or that." He held his breath.

IT'D BEEN a long time since she'd felt like this. Let herself feel like this. Excited, scared, hopeful.

Ready to trust someone.

Ready to trust the man who stopped to help a kitten. Who obviously treasured the memory of his first love, his first cat, and wasn't afraid to show it.

Who seemed to really like her, too, for *herself*.

"Yes," she said. "Yes."

She had a feeling more than just the kitten's life had changed today.

# KNITTING INTO LOVE

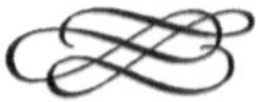

*L*ydia glared at her monitor, a free-standing 26" behemoth taking up a good chunk of real estate on her dumpster-dived heavy oak desk.

That monitor made her Macbook still usable.

Even with reading glasses, she had a hard time with the 13" laptop screen.

But it didn't matter *what* glasses she wore, she wasn't liking the numbers she was looking at on the spreadsheet.

That pattern repeat just wouldn't work across all the sizes of the sweater she was designing. She could do fewer sizes, still starting at a 30" bust and going up to 60", but she wouldn't get to size the sweater for every two inches like she wanted. And the damn pattern was due to the online magazine tonight.

She'd promised it by tonight, and she didn't break promises.

Lydia sipped her coffee (black as sin, thank you very much, with beans she roasted and ground herself, and brewed with a simple pour over apparatus), from her favorite mug. The cream-colored mug was decorated with embossed traditional knitted cabled patterns, cabled diamonds and braids and bumpy seed stitch.

She'd picked that mug up ten years ago on her only visit to

Rhinebeck, the preeminent sheep and fiber festival in the entire country, held yearly in the fall in upstate New York. Officially it was the New York State Sheep and Wool Festival, but everyone called it Rhinebeck after the quaint town that hosted the festival.

She could still remember the taste of the apple cider donuts she splurged on both mornings, nibbling while strolling through the stall-filled low-eaved red barns, shuffling through straw and checking out all the different sheep breeds.

The tiny friendly Shetland sheep, barely knee high to her (and she was short, five two on a good day), were her favorites, with their sweet faces and curled horns and wool ranging from creamy white to black.

Lydia had since carried a line of Shetland yarn, a veritable rainbow of heathered colors that filled the wooden cubbyholes along one wall of Cozy Me Cozy Ewe. She hadn't been able to go to Rhinebeck again, couldn't afford the time or cash in traveling clear across the country, even if it was a tax write off as a business expense. But the Shetland yarn reminded her of the festival, the donuts, the cider, the earthy smell of the sheep, the brilliant orange and red leaves of fall that she never saw here in Santa Cruz.

But as much as she loved the fall foliage, she loved the beach, the ocean, more than any pretty oak leaves. And it *did* get cold enough to wear sweaters, especially in the winter or on late night beach walks any time of the year.

Add a stranded knitting class to the spring line up. Stranded knits, worked with at least two yarns, were especially cozy. She hadn't taught a stranded knitting class in a while, and the Shetland yarn was perfect for it, whether someone wanted to work up a traditionally patterned fair isle hat or do something funky, like a motif of trash diving raccoons or surfboards. She had a couple patterns she designed herself that would be great first time projects.

The bell hooked to the glass front door of the shop jangled, and Lydia peered over her monitor.

Pine wooden racks lined both the walls of her store, stuffed full of yarn organized by fiber and weight (from thin strands of lace weight yarn to thick bulky yarn). The center of the store held several thrift-store wooden tables she'd stripped and waxed. Upon these she'd set baskets of bagged fiber for spinning, various knitting accessories like pom pom makers, and packets of knitting needles.

She could see the whole store from her desk. If someone needed help, she could stop whatever she was working on; but if they seemed fine just browsing, she could stay at her desk and still keep an eye on them.

This person looked like he'd need help. He had a full head of silver-touched brown hair and laugh lines around his eyes. Dark jeans with blue suede driving moccasins peeking out underneath. A trim-fitting chambray shirt, sleeves rolled up to exposed muscular forearms and a leather-banded Apple watch.

And tall! Six feet at least.

Her age, Lydia bet, at least mid forties, maybe even a very fit fifty something.

Men like him came in shopping for their wife.

Sure, there were male knitters. Most were young and hip. Some of the most popular knitting designers were flamboyant millennial men.

Not silver foxes like this guy.

"Hi," she said, standing up. "Welcome to Cozy Me Cozy Ewe. Can I help you find something?"

He smiled. Ooh, nice white teeth. It was a quirk of hers but she did like a nice smile. Her dad, rest in peace, had been a dentist, and the only thing she knew as well as yarn was dental hygiene.

"I hope so," he said. "I got stranded by work for a few extra days, and I didn't pack any WIPs."

At first Lydia heard *whips*. And her brain dived down into her nether regions. Nice smile and some kink underneath all that denim?

Ooh la *la*.

She didn't hear *WIPs*, works in progress, a common knitting term.

And then she realized what he had really said. *WIP*. And she blushed beet red.

As he continued smiling at her, his eyes growing more puzzled.

~

ETHAN PACE GLANCED at his watch before entering Cozy Me Cozy Ewe. Open til 7 p.m. He had just enough time to shop for some yarn and needles before dinner.

The meeting with the start up over the hill in San Jose had gotten postponed til Monday, and he couldn't wrap his head around flying back to New York tonight just to fly back in two days.

He hadn't visited Santa Cruz since he was a teenager wanting to re-live *Lost Boys*. (As Kiefer, not Jason Patric, and without the antlers at the end.)

A weekend here could be fun.

But that meant he had to do some quick shopping. He usually always traveled with a knitting project, socks or mittens or a hat, something small, but he'd just finished a pair of socks the other day and hadn't cast on for another project yet.

Yeah, to some people it might seem weird that a fifty-mumble-mumble guy knit, especially one more known for Angel investments, but he loved making something useful, something *real*. Not just moving money around and making people richer than any one person really deserved.

Knitting filled that purpose for him.

The bell dangling from the glass door jangled as he entered the store.

He breathed in. Lavender and lanolin. Nice. The store *was* cozy, yarn stuffing cubbies along the side walls, and all the necessary knitting accoutrements filling wicker baskets along scuffed wooden tables in the center of the small store. Wooden ladder-backed chairs lined those tables as well, and he bet the proprietor taught classes. Or at least encouraged patrons to hang out and knit. A couple cocoa colored upholstered chairs sat in the corner to the left, near a small rack of magazines (Vogue Knitting, Interweave Knits, Pom Pom Quarterly) and books, stitch dictionaries and pattern collections.

He wished he had more time to browse, to even just sit and knit, but he had dinner reservations at a tiny bistro that was due to get a

Michelin star the next time those guys came through this area. One of the reasons he'd decided to stay the weekend.

And the store was only open til seven anyways.

A woman stood up from behind a monitor taking up most of the space on an oversized vintage oak desk. He hadn't even seen her when he came in.

Gosh, she was short. Five foot if he guessed right. But adorable. Long silver curly hair held off her face by black-rimmed reading glasses sitting on top of her head. Pale luminescent skin that spoke of judicious use of sunscreen, but old enough for laugh lines at the corners of her bright green eyes. She wore snug fitting jeans and a peridot green knitted lace camisole that he bet she'd made herself.

"Hi," she said, her voice husky and rich. "Welcome to Cozy Me Cozy Ewe. Can I help you find something?"

Oh, boy, he certainly hoped so. He hoped he wasn't staring, but she was the sexiest woman he'd seen in a long time. That voice. Those eyes.

He smiled. He always smiled when he was nervous, he couldn't help it, a big ear to ear grin.

"I hope so," he said. "I got stranded by work for a few extra days, and I didn't pack any WIPs."

She stared back at him, face turning beet red.

Ethan kept smiling. Did he say something wrong? What did he say? Oh, god, say *something*.

"I like knitting socks," he said. He glanced around. One section of one wall was all Shetland yarn. Nice! Most stores didn't carry Shetland. It was very wooly, not as soft as the more common Merino and Merino blends. He walked over to the bins and picked up a skein of rich heathery indigo Shetland. Smelled it. Lanolin and hay. He could picture the sheep, with their cute little faces and plush coats. If he ever bought land and needed an agricultural tax write off, he'd get a flock of Shetland sheep. Forget alpacas (a pyramid scheme if he'd ever seen one). Shetland sheep and a border collie.

He stroked the yarn. It was soft and springy and he could picture the socks, ribbed with just a row of cream at the top and cream for the heel and toe. The rest that gorgeous indigo. Easy enough knitting, but it would let the yarn shine.

"You knit?" the woman asked, walking over to the Shetland yarn as well.

He stopped smiling. "Um, yes."

"No, I mean, I thought you were shopping for someone else, for your wife—"

"Because men don't knit?"

"I know plenty of men who knit, they just don't look like you...." Her face flushed again.

He raised an eyebrow. "What do they look like?"

"Younger, I mean, more hip, oh crap...."

*SHUT UP, shut up, shut up, Lydia!*

"Can I start over?" she asked. "I'm Lydia. I usually don't stick my foot quite so deep down my throat."

Her face felt hot enough to set the store on fire.

*Shut* up! What was she thinking?

She knew quite well what she was thinking, and it was all R-rated at best.

"I'm Ethan," he said, his voice a warm baritone that rumbled through her. He held out his hand. "And I really truly knit."

She shook his hand briskly. Didn't want to let go. His hand was warm, with just a touch of roughness. He'd need some hand lotion or he'd snag the yarn.

He held her hand just long enough to have her wanting more. Much more.

"I'm sorry I presumed," she said.

Gosh, that sounded...pretentious.

He shrugged. "Not the first time someone has judged me."

"I'm sorry—"

"And there's no wife." He smiled.

And her face had just been cooling off. No wife? That opened up possibilities.

"No girlfriend. No boyfriend or husband either for that matter," he added, smiling even more.

Oh, those teeth. She could run her tongue along them. Other places too.

"Me neither."

"Help me pick out some yarn and some needles then come to dinner with me," he said.

HE WAS GRINNING SO HARD his jaw ached. But he'd done it! He'd asked her to dinner. It had been years since he'd even wanted to spend time with a woman. He couldn't let this opportunity go. Not with how her hand had felt in his. Even if she was a shop owner in Santa Cruz, and he lived in New York, and he knew nothing could come of it—

"I, um—" She scrunched her nose. "I have a pattern I'm working on."

"Oh." Five minutes. How could five minutes and even less conversation make him feel kicked in the gut?

"Okay, then, I'll take three skeins of the blue, and one of the cream. Do you have size 0 circular needles?" he said, voice flat.

"Not in stock here at the store," she said. "I'm sorry. I have some size 1 circs."

"Won't work for me." He tucked the Shetland skeins back into the cubbies.

She gulped. Looked down. "I can loan you mine. I'm not planning on any projects requiring them anytime soon."

"I can't take your needles."

"You'd give them back, right? Next time you're in town?"

He looked around the store. Looked back at her, with her green eyes wide. Maybe she did feel something too. "Of course. I promise."

He smiled. This time real, not nervous. "I knit fast, though. I can get those socks done in a week. You might be seeing me sooner than you think."

"I really do have a pattern due. I'm having some issues with it. It'll take at least an hour or two. I wish I could go to dinner with you," she said in a rush. "But I have to get it done. I promised."

"So you're just busy tonight?" he asked.

Lydia nodded.

"Dinner tomorrow?" He was already texting the restaurant. They'd get him in tomorrow. He hated to pull strings, but in this case...

"I—yes. Yes."

"Great. Are you working tomorrow?"

"Every day."

"Can I pick up the yarn and needles in the morning? And then we can figure out everything else." He watched her anxiously.

"Everything else?" she asked, then smiled. "Yes. That sounds really good."

ETHAN LEFT Cozy Me Cozy You after that. She'd locked the door after him and turned the sign to CLOSED and pulled down the shades. She worked best at the store, not at home.

And sure enough, an hour and two mugs of coffee later she realized, if she tweaked just *this* with the main stitch pattern, and then *that*, with the side panels...the numbers all worked out.

She retrieved her knitting needle clutch out of the bottom drawer of the desk. Pulled out the size 0 circs. Set them on top of her desk for tomorrow.

It would all work out.

# COWBOY BOOTS AND TACOS

*K*ate squished her toes in her sneakers. It hardly ever snowed in Austin, Texas, not even in mid December, but someone on 37th Street had splurged on a snow machine and created a small pile of crunchy snow in their postage-stamp sized front yard. That plus the light drizzle of cold rain equaled slush, already muddy and melting.

Melting into her sneakers and soaking her thin cotton socks.

She didn't own any winter boots. Just dress cowboy boots for going out dancing, black leather with red and turquoise inlays, a college graduation gift from her dad Clay. UC Berkeley Class of '89. He'd been so proud.

Her house was a 1920s Tudor, just 850 square feet of vintage quirkiness and creaky oak floors, sparsely furnished with her dad's furniture. Pieces he'd crafted himself, plus the old leather couch with the Hereford brown and white cowhide cushions that he'd had since she was a child. Hideous, but he'd loved it. And so did Kate.

Kate didn't have room for extra things. Not shoes, not anything. Layla, a fellow grad student in the Zoology department at the University of Texas, and Kate's housemate and best friend, didn't mind a bit of clutter. But it was Kate's house.

And there was no way she was going to risk ruining those cowboy boots, anyways. Wet feet were a small price.

She shoved her bare hands into the snug front pockets of her soft worn blue jeans, willing her fingertips warm. Her breath puffed in the deepening twilight, and she breathed in the exhaust of the line of cars trundling down the narrow street, their occupants too wimpy to walk the quirky neighborhood to see the lights.

Oh, who could blame them. Her blonde hair under her knitted wool beanie was darkened to brunette by the drizzle, and her light weight running jacket layered over a turtleneck did little to keep the chill off her lean runner's torso.

Kate eyed the jaunty black silk top hat stuck on top of the slumped pile of manmade snow, the dirty red and green striped scarf crumpled along the base. Hand-painted maroon and red Christmas lights were draped haphazardly over the branches of the gnarled live oak that took most of the front yard, coloring the snow a sullen blood red. A tattered cardboard sign duct taped to a wooden stake, stabbed through the center of the pile, read BAH HUMBUG.

Beady brown pecans for eyes on either side of a twisted dry carrot nose stared at her blankly.

*Merry fricking Christmas.*

37th Street, an eclectic community north of the University of Texas campus, was filled with small clapboard houses and yards full of weeds and live oak trees, and populated by a mix of old hippies and UT students.

Every year some of the residents chose to decorate for the holiday. Decorating wasn't mandatory, of course. But most people got into the spirit.

But their Christmas decorations were not the normal store-bought plywood and wire yard contraptions.

Store-bought was anathema.

That meant you got some interesting takes on the holidays.

"Wow, that's dark," Layla said, joining Kate on the cracked sidewalk, kicking aside a clump of melting snow. Layla wore a cozy cream-colored wool sweater, unfaded jeans, and LL Bean rubber and leather boots. She had braided her dark hair into two long plaits, with festive red bows securing the ends.

"Frosty killed by global warming per Al Gore? Gen X ennui? What's next, Rudolph being barbequed?" Layla continued.

"Don't give anyone ideas," Kate said. She *did* smell barbeque, a succulent meaty odor overlaid by the rich tang of mesquite smoke. Her mouth watered. Some entrepreneur might be selling brisket tacos at one of the houses. She had a spare couple bucks. Sort of. She could splurge on a taco.

They walked to the next house, catching a whiff of marijuana wafting from the ajar front door. Austin. Someone living the slacker's lifestyle. A 1960s VW van was parked kitty-corner across the front yard, thirty years plus of rust and primer paint dotting its cream and mint green body. A taxidermy armadillo with angel wings sat in the driver's seat, nestled amidst plush silver tinsel garlands and white lights blinking in time with a theremin version of Silent Night playing on a glitter-encrusted cassette player.

"It's kinda pretty," said Layla.

"In a weird way," agreed Kate. *More dead things.* The armadillo did have a sweet expression. Poor little Texas speed bump.

After that was a house that invited folks into the backyard via a gravel path softly lit by paper bag luminarias. Different dioramas were tucked under and around the cactus and agaves. A toy plastic Tyrannosaur wearing a knitted Santa hat menaced a mock up of the state capitol, little paper bats attached to wires dangling above its head. A company of green Army men assaulted a rosemary bush Christmas tree with miniature ornaments rather than weapons, with one soldier topping the bush with a star. A pack of plush toy dogs, beagles and spaniels and shepherds, tilted their noses to howl at a paper mâché cheddar cheese moon, Santa and his sleigh silhouetted against the orange craters.

Kate smiled at the dogs despite herself.

The next house was a rainbow of lights, strands running through the chicken wire geometric shapes that dangled and twirled from a huge oak tree. One large dodecahedron, easily ten feet across, came within a couple feet of the ground. You could crawl under it and reach up and spin it. Layla and Kate waited their turn to lie down under the oak on the blue plastic tarp, to stare up through the spinning lights and bare branches to the velvety sky above.

This was the house, too, with the barbeque. And sure enough, someone was selling tacos in the backyard, the side gate to the backyard open and welcoming.

Kate bought two tacos, one for her, one for Layla, from a sweet-faced young man she vaguely recognized from around campus. Glossy dark hair pulled back into a short ponytail, bright green eyes, dressed in jeans and an orange puffy down jacket. Fellow grad student, different department?

"We're raising some money to offset the electricity," he said, his voice lacking any Texas twang. More like the Californian non-accent Kate recognized from undergrad at Berkeley. He gestured to the electric meter mounted on the side of the clapboard house. The meter was outlined by yellow lights, its dial spinning madly. "Whatever I make off donations, we're sharing with all the houses."

A rickety folding table under the meter held plastic bins with condiments, metal tongs and ladles, and paper napkins. She grabbed pickled red onions and jalapenos and a handful of napkins, then, with just a twinge, stuffed a twenty into the coffee can next to a bin of salsa. That was her food budget for the week, but it was okay. These folks were putting on this display for everyone.

The taco was better than okay. The brisket was tender, and the jalapeno had just the right amount of heat. She swiped a trickle of juice off her chin and wondered if her twenty earned her another taco. Even just a small one. She glanced back.

"Here you go," the man said, holding out another taco. "I recognize that look. Tacos. Must eat tacos."

"Thanks," Kate said.

"Brian," he said. "Thank you, Brian."

Kate smiled despite herself. "Thank you, Brian."

"You're welcome—" he said.

"Kate."

"Kate. Come back for thirds later if you want." He smiled, teeth bright in the Christmas lights.

"I'll be sure to send her back," Layla said, tugging Kate towards the next house.

"Layla!" Kate hissed. She could feel her cheeks heating. The only part of her warm, though the drizzle had finally stopped. They did need to get walking again.

An hour later they were done exploring.

Layla gazed wistfully back down the brightly-lit street, at the multicolored strands of twinkling lights zig-zagging above. The groups of people laughing, enjoying the displays.

"We could still put up a tree. I have a fake one we could use. Maybe a garland for the fireplace mantel," Layla said quietly.

"I thought we agreed we could skip this year," Kate said, her throat suddenly tight. Too soon. Too *soon*.

Up to two years ago, Kate adored Christmas.

She wasn't religious, it wasn't that, but she had always loved the season. The rituals her dad Clay had created when she was a kid, and added to once she was back in Texas.

It was just the two of them, but her dad made sure the holiday was special.

Cutting down a tree, decorating it with the ornaments she had crafted over the years, from cotton ball snow men to acrylic-painted balsa wood sleds and reindeer, with pieces that fit together.

Watching *Die Hard* on the VCR, the reflections of the tree lights glittering against the glass screen. Clay loved movies, and he had amassed a library of videotapes. But *Die Hard* was his only Christmas movie.

Drinking homemade eggnog, made weeks before with eggs from Clay's flock of hens, spiked with Wild Turkey. Clay taught her how to make it. How to be patient, 'cause even with fresh eggs, he said you had to let it age.

But now she had no family.

Less said about her mama, the better. Kate hadn't heard from Lynda since she ran off with the lead guitarist in a honky-tonk band when Kate was eight years old. Kate didn't care if Lynda was alive or dead, to be frank. Didn't keep in touch with anyone from that half of the family.

Her grandparents, Clay's parents, were long gone, as was Clay's much older sister Betty Jo. Kate had only met Betty Jo a couple times, as a child. Betty Jo was aloof, with cold blue eyes and knifelike cheekbones that made her look gaunt. Clay had those cheekbones, but he had laugh lines that brightened his face.

Then Clay had to up and die, two years ago. Just two days before Christmas. Willard Jones had come by to exercise his Palomino quarter horse mare, and found Clay sprawled over a bale of hay, cold and stiff.

Not even fifty years old.

Kate had been planning a big 50th bash, just after New Year's, as a surprise. Clay was well loved in the community. He'd touched a lot of lives. Everyone was excited about the party.

Instead she hosted a memorial service Christmas Eve. Settled Clay's affairs, not there was much for her to do. Her daddy always had things arranged just so. She got that from him. Sold the ranch and the small herd of Hereford cattle he'd kept for tax purposes.

She had enough left over to buy the brick Tudor in Austin, as long as she was frugal and had a roommate. Hyde Park was a historic neighborhood. If she got lucky, the home would be a good investment. If not, the house was full of quirky Austin character.

Got back to school and her job as a teaching assistant just in time. Both calendar time and heart heavy time. She needed to throw herself into work. Keep busy. Not think. At least, not think about her dad.

Thank all the gods for Layla. Initially just someone Kate nodded to as they went to their respective labs in the Zoology department, they grew to be best friends. It was a given Layla would move in, when Kate bought the house. Kate owed Layla for her love and support after Clay passed. She'd nursed Layla through a couple break ups, the last a sweet-talking cowboy with wandering boots and a nice behind in his tight fitting jeans. But it wasn't the same.

Kate hadn't truly come up for air til now.

This year, getting out and seeing the lights on 37th Street was as much as she could stomach right now, regarding Christmas. It was something that she'd never done with Clay, so it was different enough. And Layla had persisted.

Kate didn't want a Christmas tree in her house. Not even a darn garland. Too close to those happier memories.

But maybe Layla was right. It *had* been two years. The ache was dulling.

"Okay," Kate said. "We can do your tree. But only if you get me a scoop of Amy's Mexican Vanilla on the walk back home."

"Oh, that's easy!" Layla said, her smile bright.

IT WASN'T EVEN nine p.m. when they got back to their house. Walking to Amy's was the wrong direction from 37th Street. They'd earned their ice cream.

Layla got to work the minute they got into the house.

"We can put the tree right in front of the living room window," she said, excited. "It will look so pretty. Can you move the couch? I'll be right back."

Kate stared at her living room. There wasn't much furniture: her dad's old couch, the rectangular oak coffee table he'd made, and a thrifted green velvet bucket chair. The limestone fireplace took up most of one wall, white painted built-ins filled with books on either side of it.

The couch was in front of the large window with its wavy glass panes.

That was where it belonged, in all its brown and white cow spotted glory.

Though it might be nice opposite the fireplace. She could shift the chair over.

Things *did* change. Didn't have to be bad.

She shoved the couch opposite the fireplace, then went to the kitchen to get a broom and dustpan. Holy cow, that was a lot of dust bunnies!

The phone, mounted to the dining room wall next to the kitchen door, rang.

"I'll get it," Kate yelled, then "Hello?"

"Hi. Kate Burnham?"

"Speaking," Kate said.

"I'm going to apologize in advance. This is a little awkward. Are you the daughter of Clay Burnham?"

"Yes," said Kate cautiously.

"My name is Maria Ramos. I'm a genealogist working for the Defense POW/MIA Accounting Agency. I have information about your grandparents. Do you know who your grandfather was? And your grandmother?"

"Ralph Burnham was my grandpa. Rita was my grandma. I mean, my dad always said Ralph adopted him, but he considered Ralph his dad. Apparently his biological dad died in World War Two. My grandparents never talked about him, though. Even my dad didn't know his name."

"Honey, your grandpa's name was Clayton Gunsauls, born in 1921 in Pennsylvania. And yes, he did die in World War Two. He was on the flight crew of a plane that went down in the North Sea in November 1943 after the bombing of Bremen."

"Oh, wow. That's—thanks for letting me know. We never had a name."

"Your grandma was Betty Jo Richards."

Kate felt dizzy. "Betty Jo was my aunt."

"I have a marriage certificate from February 1943 from Boise, Idaho, for Clayton Gunsauls and Betty Jo Richards. And a birth certificate for January 1944 for a Clay Gunsauls, son of Clayton and Betty Jo. It took me a bit of tracking down to find out what happened to baby Clay, but it looks like Rita adopted him as her own son. Once Ralph adopted him, baby Clay was Clay Burnham, not Clay Gunsauls."

Kate leaned against the wall. It made sense, in a world tilted askew sort of way. Her dad had talked about his early childhood years in Boise before they all moved to Texas.

Talked about his older sister Betty Jo, too, when twelve year old Kate asked about her, after the last time Kate ever saw her. She and Clay had been visiting her grandparents a couple years before Rita passed. Betty Jo stopped in briefly.

Clay told Kate about how they never got along. How he hardly ever saw her, growing up.

Layla lugged a large cardboard box past her, then stopped. "Are you okay? Let me put this down."

Kate waved her along, mouthed, *It's okay.*

Maria Ramos echoed that. "Are you okay, Kate? I know this might be a shock."

"Can you send me anything on this? Copies of the certificates, anything?"

"I'm not supposed to, but—"

"Please? My dad died two Christmases ago."

Brief silence. "I'm sorry about that. I did find his death certificate. I can mail you photocopies. Just don't tell anyone."

Kate's throat tightened. "Did Clayton Gunsauls come from a big family?"

"He did," Maria said, her voice soft. "He was the youngest of two brothers, and he had a younger sister too. His parents passed in the 1960s, but you have a host of second and third cousins."

"I don't know what to say."

"If any remains need to be identified, the agency may contact you for a DNA sample. You're Clayton Gunsauls' last living descendant."

"Wow. I don't quite know what to feel. How am I supposed to feel?" Kate said. "Here's my address."

"Merry Christmas, honey. I'll get that info out to you. I found a copy of a photo from his obituary. Sweet picture of him in uniform with the family dog. I'll send that too."

"Thanks," Kate said. She hung up.

"Kate, sweetie, are you okay?" Layla rushed over and hugged her. "Katie, who was that?"

"Someone working for the Department of Defense or something. A genealogist looking for the descendents of service members. I found out my biological grandpa's name," Kate said. A sob hitched in her throat. "And who my grandma was." She told Layla the details.

"And," Kate concluded, "I have cousins. I don't know if I'll ever look them up, but it's kind of neat to know I have family out there. But you know what? If Betty Jo was my grandma, she never cared about me. She only saw me a couple times. I was her granddaughter, and she didn't care."

"Sweetie, you have family right here. Me," Layla said. "Don't ever doubt that. I love you. Your dad loved you. Family isn't just blood. You know that. Look at the love your grandfather had for your dad. They weren't blood. Family is who you choose."

Kate nodded. "I know that, I do, but…."

"Let me pour you some eggnog. It's store bought, but I got some of that Wild Turkey so I can make it like your dad's tasted. Sort of, anyways. And let's put up the tree."

Layla unpacked the big box. "Voila!" she said, standing the tree up and plugging in the base.

The five foot tall silver tree. With a lighted base: sky blue and dandelion yellow and buttermint pink lights. And the tree revolved, reflecting the pastel candy colors off the ceiling like a Christmas disco ball.

Kate's sobs turned to hiccups. "Oh good lord," she gasped. "You've got to be kidding me."

"This tree was my grandmama's," Layla said proudly, standing back to look at it. "I have some vintage glass bulbs I usually decorate it with, but we can use whatever you'd like. And then we'll watch *Die Hard*."

Kate reached for Layla and hugged her. "Thank you," she whispered.

~

KATE WOKE up late the next day. Too much eggnog. Or too much bourbon, rather, too late into the early morning hours.

She puttered to the kitchen to make coffee. Layla had left a note: *Gotta go to the lab. Lights again, tonight? Meet me by the spinning lights tree at seven p.m. and we'll grab dinner after, my treat.*

The ridiculous silver tinsel tree looked great, even unplugged, in the early afternoon winter sunshine streaming through the big window. They'd decorated the tree with a mix of Layla's glass bulbs and Kate's old ornaments. She was glad Layla had convinced her about the tree. Even about the eggnog.

Maybe she could go get a fresh garland and put it across the wide mantel. The pine scent would be refreshing. Then go for a run by Town Lake, shower, walk over to 37th Street, and meet up with Layla.

The afternoon went as planned. Kate found comfort in that. And felt a bit of anticipation. The night promised to be dry, no drizzle or rain. She pulled on her nicest jeans and her black cowboy boots. Topped it with an embroidered long-sleeved Western shirt and Clay's old fringed suede jacket.

Even a dash of peppermint flavored, pink tinted lip balm, instead of the plain old Chapstick.

She walked over to 37th Street a little after six, starting again at the house with the melted Frosty. He'd been rebuilt, snow packed into three neat balls, with a fresh carrot for his nose. His new sign read *HAPPY HOLIDAYS!* And the red lights didn't look murderous any more. Just Christmas-y.

Even the armadillo in the VW van didn't look quite as tattered.

And she could smell brisket again.

One taco. One taco wouldn't ruin her dinner.

And maybe Brian would be there. First time in a long time she'd even felt the bit of interest for someone.

She walked through the gate to the backyard, smiling.

Then stopped.

It wasn't Brian.

Oh, the guy slicing brisket was just as cute, maybe cuter, with twinkling blue eyes and bright red hair and a sandy beard to make a Viking proud.

But not Brian.

She backed away, ignoring his cheery wave. Her chest tightened.

She'd thought she was okay. She thought she'd processed everything. She dashed at her eyes.

Not in public. She wouldn't break down in public.

It was early enough there wasn't anyone waiting to lay on the tarp under the oak and look up at the lights and the darkening sky.

She scooched under the low hanging dodecahedron and laid down. If she cried now, no one could see her. She reached up and spun the contraption, the lights like neon comets against the branches of the oak and the night sky above. One tear trickled, warm against her cool face. She let it stripe her cheek. Stretching out her arms to either side, she touched dried grass and cold dirt, just beyond the tarp. She dug her fingers in, letting herself sink against the earth.

Breathe in, breathe out.

Barbeque. The rich meaty smell, and the funk of the mesquite tamed by the vanilla of pecan wood.

Listen.

Folks walking by, laughing, chattering. The creepy beautiful theremin beyond that, "Silent Night" segueing to "Amazing Grace".

The earth warmed under her fingertips.

The plastic tarp rustled. Someone touched her hand gently.

"I was hoping I'd see you again. I'm saving a taco for you." He left his hand resting against hers. Not taking. Just there.

Brian.

She entwined her fingers with his.

"I'm going out to dinner in a bit with my best friend. But, yeah, I'd like a taco."

# CABERNET KISSES

As soon as Rachael drove into the wine country town of St Helena, her hands relaxed on the steering wheel of her rust-and-red '05 Z4 Beemer.

White holiday lights festooned the ficus trees lining the sidewalks, twinkling against the dark sky. More lights trimmed the windows and awnings of the restaurants, galleries and boutiques that occupied the brick and stucco buildings of Main Street, adding to the holiday cheer. She loved the holiday lights. Wished they could stay up all year.

Some of those buildings dated back to the late 1800s. Decades older than the Spanish Revival bungalow she'd inherited from her bachelor uncle Jay. She loved old houses, but it was the town, that restored rather than ripped down buildings, that convinced her to fix up her bungalow, rather than sell it.

She lowered the driver's side window a couple inches, smelling wood smoke from fireplaces. A rare hint of snow, minerally and sharp, tickled her tongue, and she closed the window reluctantly. Her worn ribbed cashmere sweater, the navy fabric pilled and the elbows darned, kept her warm enough despite the clunky on again, off again car heater. But not warm enough to keep the windows down. Not with the thin canvas of her Beemer's rag top.

Rachael could now forget about her caseload of cancer patients (or at least put them in the back of her mind—she could never really forget them, not even that rotten little landshark Tabasco, Mr. Jensen's tea cup Chihuahua) for the next week.

Oh, she needed this break. Why did everyone's pet get *sicker* at the holidays?

An emergency consult on a golden retriever, with relapsing lymphoma, kept her from leaving Los Angeles at 6 a.m. as she'd originally planned. The dog, Honey, was as sweet as her name, with equally charming owners. Rachael didn't think Honey had much time left, but she'd done her best that morning to make sure what time Honey did have was comfortable.

Sometimes that was all she could do.

So she was rolling into St Helena at 6:40 p.m., instead of early afternoon. Ah well. That gentle kiss on her hand from Honey made it all worth it.

Rachael had planned to hit the Home Depot in Napa, picking up the supplies she'd need for working on her bungalow this week, on her way north to St Helena. Stopping at Sunshine Market for the week's groceries, once she got to town.

Then off load supplies into the detached garage, put away groceries, and unpack. Shower. Enjoy a glass of Cabernet. Organize her thoughts for the week ahead.

Then let her friend Jamie drag her to the annual holiday party Jamie was hosting for her winery clients. Jamie had insisted. Rachael had to go to the party. No begging off that she was tired, or had to work on the house.

That was the plan.

That plan was kaput. Home Depot and grocery shopping got moved to tomorrow. She'd grab an English muffin at Model for breakfast, instead of cooking in.

The party, really more of a cocktail hour, had started at six. Jamie didn't expect it to go much longer than eight: even though it was a Friday night, most of her clients were working Saturday. That meant Rachael didn't have time to stop at the bungalow to change, let alone unpack.

She'd have to change in the bathroom at the venue.

At Jamie's request (*order*, amended Rachael), Rachael had packed the only sorta fancy dress she owned: a long slinky sheath dress she'd picked up on clearance a couple years ago and worn twice. The dress wasn't at all wintery—the print was bright orange poppies against a cream background—but it would have to do. Rachael lived in scrubs. No point in buying clothes she wouldn't wear. All her extra cash was going into the bungalow.

And, she had to admit, into the barely formed dream of selling her oncology practice to her bright eyed and perky associate Dr Kim, just a couple years out of his residency. She loved her job, but twenty years into it, she'd already weathered a couple episodes of near burn out.

Yes, selling the practice, and using the cash to start a palliative care mobile practice in Napa Valley, sounded better and better every day.

Her phone's directions app directed her to turn right off Main Street, then a quick left. Jamie had booked the tasting room in a wine bar for her shindig. The address was for a standalone two story stone building, housing several businesses. The Limehouse wine bar was at the far end, with two big multi-paned windows on either side of a red Dutch door.

She could see figures milling about through the wavy glass of the windows.

There was no way she was going to sneak in so she could change clothes. Not without waltzing past all the guests.

Maybe there was a back entrance. She turned down a narrow gravel driveway to the back of the building, her tires crunching, then squeezed her car into a narrow space between a fancy black pickup and a white Tesla sport utility.

Good thing the Beemer was tiny.

And she didn't care if anyone dinged her doors. That ship had sailed ten years plus ago.

She fished her dress out of her carryon sized suitcase, along with a combo strapless bra/shapewear thing she needed to even shimmy into the darn dress. Grabbed the pair of tan sandals that she suspected she would only wear once, this trip. Tonight.

And finally, a tube of mascara.

She had to, at least, not *totally* embarrass Jamie.

There *was* a back door, a nondescript steel industrial door, bearing a token holiday wreath of pine boughs and red ribbons. And it was unlocked. *And* it opened into a empty hallway that likely serviced all the businesses. The bathroom was the first door on the right. She could change, drop off her jeans, loafers, and sweater into the Beemer, then go around to the front. No one would be the wiser.

*Here,* she texted Jamie. *Changing. Be right there.*

Josh parked his pickup in the gravel lot behind the Limehouse wine bar, leaving plenty of room between his pickup and Dick Reinhart's new Tesla sport utility. Dick, one of the nicest guys in the Valley, babied that vehicle. Josh didn't want to risk dinging the Tesla.

Late. Josh hated being late. But he'd lost track of time, working on spreadsheets in his office above the Endicott Winery tasting room. He'd grabbed an old tweed jacket and ran out the door, not even stopping to piss on his way out.

Something he should've taken care of, as his bladder reminded him.

He grabbed the case of wine from the truck bed. Might as well get something accomplished out of going to this party. Jamie had requested he drop off a mixed case for her to schlep to a new restaurant in downtown Napa sometime this week. Now seemed like a good time.

If the restaurant liked it, they might feature it in their wine list.

Endicott Winery could use that. Another steady source of revenue? Oh, yes.

But going to a *party….* he had a ton of work at the winery, planning for next year, never mind deciding what to do with some juice that he didn't particularly want to use in his own wine, but wasn't sure if anyone else would want it at this point.

Stop. Just stop. Take the time for a breather. Jamie had insisted he take the time to relax on her dime for a couple hours. And she'd been great to him and Endicott over the past couple years.

He owed it to her to show up and be social. Wasn't like he didn't know everyone, and he did like most of them.

Drop off the wine, say hello, then visit the bathroom.

Quickly.

RACHAEL BARGED INTO THE BATHROOM. The tiny room smelled of lavender and bleach disinfectant. It had a sink and toilet, nothing else, not even a small table. The polished concrete floor and black-grouted white subway tile walls added up to vintage industrial wine country style. The white porcelain sink, mounted to the wall, looked original at her quick glance.

Stop checking out the fixtures. She had to hurry.

She hung the dress off the purse hook next to the sink by one spaghetti strap, and tucked the shapewear through the armhole. Two paper towels on the floor for her to stand on, one per each foot. The floor looked clean, but it *was* a public bathroom.

She put her loafers in the sink, then folded her jeans on top of them, followed by undies, sweater, and bra.

She caught a glimpse of herself in the mirror. Curves (some *not* in the right places). But muscles, too. Not bad for late forties, given she hardly had time to work out. Not with the hours the practice demanded.

Time to yank on the shapewear. How could something that looked like a modest beige bathing suit be so *evil*? She squirmed and tugged and jumped until she got the bra top covering her boobs.The paper towels for her feet were in shreds by the end.

She always felt like a fat seal, all her curves encased in a smooth layer. No wonder she'd only worn the dumb dress twice. She stepped into the sandals, then tugged the dress over her head, her arms straight up. Worse than a straight jacket. She wriggled her torso.

Not that she'd ever worn a straight jacket, but worse than she imagined *it* would be.

The door handle clicked.

Rachael froze. She'd locked it, right? Right?

She tugged faster, getting her arms free, the dress still bunched around her boobs, and turned toward the door.

And watched in horror, speechless, as the door knob *turned*.

And the door opened, revealing a stocky, muscular man in neat jeans, white button down shirt, and a tweed sports jacket. He wore thick horn rimmed glasses that did nothing to hide the bright blue of his eyes. He had a bit of gray at his temples, but his dark brown hair was thick and shiny. His jaw dropped.

Rachael didn't know if the lurch in her stomach was humiliation or desire.

Because he was the cutest man she'd seen in years.

Saying hello hadn't been quick. Not at all. Josh thought he was going to explode before he escaped out the back door of Limehouse into the hallway with the shared bathroom. He jiggled the door knob for the bathroom.

Thank god. It was unlocked. He pushed the door open, then stopped, jaw dropping.

Because the prettiest woman he'd seen in years stood there, trapped by a silky dress lodged around her breasts, and one of those goofy Spanx underwear things around her tummy and hips.

He looked up, meeting her wide gray eyes. Wow. Between her curves and those piercing eyes....

Three years since Emily had left him. Perfectly manicured with blood red nails, perfectly coiffed with platinum blond tresses, hot yoga skinny Emily. Left him, because Josh refused to sell Endicott to one of the big labels buying up mountain vineyards. Emily was long tired of not having any of the money she saw all around her. She didn't understand Josh's love of the land. The change of seasons. The vines, the grapes, the wine he coaxed out of them.

By the time she'd left, he'd been relieved.

Way more than three years and not a spark of interest for anyone.

Until this woman.

The gray-eyed woman yanked down on the dress, trying to cover herself up.

They both blanched at the hissing rrrip.

The dress had split at one of the side seams.

OH GOD.

Rachael could suture up a biopsy site, but she had nothing to repair the dress with. And the shredded seam looked beyond her non-biological sewing skills, anyways.

Rachael glared at the man. No matter how handsome he was, this ranked up with one of the most humiliating moments in her life. On par with that day in Anatomy when she slipped on the formaldehyde slick floor and ended up with her face pressed up against the preserved belly of the horse—nay, the *stallion*, and in all his glory— they were dissecting.

AND she had nothing to wear. At this point, she needed a glass of wine, and Jamie had promised to open some nice bottles for this soiree.

Maybe more than one glass.

Definitely more than one glass. She could always take a rideshare home.

"Out, out, out!" Screw it. Jeans and sweater were fine. The man was wearing jeans (and filling them out quite nicely). All the other windows in the building had been dark. He must be here for Jamie's party.

And, oh crap, that meant she was going to see him again.

"I'm so sorry," he said. He pulled the door shut, a panicked look in his eyes as he tripped backwards.

She slumped briefly. She wouldn't cry. She hadn't cried when Honey licked her hand.

They were two adults. And hadn't she thought the shapewear covered more than a bathing suit?

But damn, she was just so, so tired.

She tugged off the dress and balled it up, stuffing it into the garbage can. She wanted to do the same with the shapewear, but it wasn't cheap. And she probably would buy another dress. Someday. Maybe.

The man was waiting at the far end of the hallway, opposite the back door.

"I'm sorry," he said again.

"My fault for not locking the door," she said stiffly. "Though knocking might have been a good idea."

"How was I to know someone was in an unlocked bathroom?"

She gritted her teeth. "I'm getting a glass of wine. Good night."

JOSH SCANNED for her as soon as he got back to the wine bar, through the crowd of winery owners and their partners. He'd already chatted with anyone he cared to. He wanted to find the gray-eyed woman again.

Apologize.

The Limehouse was decorated for the holidays, with twinkle lights wrapped around the wine racks lining the walls, and red garlands looped around the arms of the central iron chandelier. A sprig of mistletoe dangled from the center of the chandelier as well. Instrumental Christmas music played softly, under the buzz of conversation. The room smelled of pine and red wine. No one wore perfume or cologne. That would interfere with the wine.

Dick Reinhart pulled Jamie under the mistletoe and planted a kiss on her cheek, to the shouts of approval from the guests.

Jamie wagged her finger at everyone, then pulled Dick's head down for a proper kiss.

Rumor had it they'd been dating. Looked like the rumors were true.

They made an attractive couple. Jamie was drop dead gorgeous, with natural kinky hair, a warm smile, and dark amber eyes, and a sunny personality that outshone her beauty. Dick had a craggy handsomeness that matched his eclectic wines. He was older than Jamie, but not by too much.

Good for them.

A small Christmas tree, decorated with hand-blown glass ornaments of wine bottles and wine glasses, filled one corner near the front window. A worn Persian rug, shades of salmon and faded teal, softened the wide oak floorboards. Two leather sectionals, positioned half on the floor, half on the rug, anchored the seating area.

The gray-eyed woman was perched at the end of one of the sectionals, clutching a thin-stemmed Cabernet glass filled with inky red wine.

She liked Cab. He could give her a bottle of Endicott Cab as an apology. He had a Reserve '09 in that case he'd brought. He snagged it from behind the bar, then wove his way to the woman.

"Can we start over?" he asked. "I was an idiot."

"Well," she said, "at least you know the right thing to say. Now."

He opened his mouth.

"Kidding, kidding," she said. "Wasn't your fault I didn't lock the door. I was just in such a rush to get here and get changed."

"I should have knocked—" he said.

"Nah. I was grumpy. And embarrassed."

"You shouldn't be. Embarassed." Josh's ears burned.

She arched an eyebrow and Josh caught his breath. Those eyes. And those curves.

He held out the bottle of wine.

"An apology," he said. "It's from my winery. Endicott. Block 3. 2009 vintage."

She took it from him, examined the label. "Spring Mountain? And 2009 was a really good year, right? I bet this is too much." She handed it back.

"Keep it," he said, not taking it. "I have more." Not a lot more, but she didn't need to know that.

"Only if we share it," she said.

OH, god, had she actually said that? *Only if we share it?* That sounded suspiciously like flirting, and she hadn't flirted since before she started the oncology practice.

Maybe it was time to find out if she could flirt again.

"I'm fine with that," he said. "I'd love that. I'm Josh, by the way. Seems like we forgot that part, right? Winemaker and owner of Endicott Winery."

"Rachael. I've been friends with Jamie since we were kids. I inherited my uncle's bungalow on Madrona a couple years ago. Just up here for a week this time, but I'm thinking of moving here permanently."

And she was. Something clicked. She didn't know if it was the rich wine in her glass, the cheerful banter around her, or the handsome man standing in front of her.

But it felt right.

Oh, moving wouldn't be immediate. She had to get everything in Los Angeles in order. Finish with her current cases. Get Dr Kim to buy the practice. Sell her house.

But fixing up the bungalow would be easier in person, that was for sure.

Yeah, that was it.

Jamie stepped over to them. She glanced at the bottle of Cab.

"2009? Nice. You're gonna replace that, right, Josh?" Jamie

smirked. "Café Canard Fou asked especially for a bottle of your Reserve."

"I—" Josh started.

She laughed. "Anyway, I was coming over to introduce the two of you, since you're my favorite two single people, but I've seen you've beat me to it."

Rachael narrowed her eyes. Jamie had set her up. Literally.

*Later*, she mouthed at Jamie.

~

JAMIE HAD SET HIM UP, Josh realized. Insisting he come to the party.

Oh, she'd tried over the years to find him a girlfriend. Failed miserably, with a queue of Emily clones.

But, as he looked at Rachael, he couldn't be mad at Jamie. Or even annoyed.

"Let's see, you found someone, so now you want everyone with someone?" he asked, nodding towards Dick, who'd come up behind Jamie and cuddled her to him.

"Yes," Jamie said. "Got me. But Rachael's my oldest friend. So I'm trusting you."

"Still here," Rachael said. "Apparently invisible, but still here."

"And Josh is good people," Jamie said to her, while Josh's ears burned. "If I didn't think of him as a brother, Dick wouldn't stand a chance."

Dick kissed the top of Jamie's curls. "You just wanted some age and seasoning."

"Yeah, that's it," Jamie said. "Now you two. Under the mistletoe. I want to see if I was right about sparks."

"She's pushy," Josh said to Rachael. "But I'm game, if you are."

~

RACHAEL'S TUMMY FLUTTERED.

"She's always been that way. Ever since we were kids. But, yeah, I'm game."

She let Josh pull her to her feet. Under the mistletoe. She tilted her head back, waiting.

She'd been waiting twenty years.

And the sparks zapped brighter and warmer than all the lights in town, as he pressed his lips to hers.

# ABOUT THE AUTHOR

Since graduating from West Point, Stephannie Tallent has served in the Army as a Military Intelligence officer during Desert Storm, gotten a Zoology degree, went to vet school, worked as a small animal veterinarian, and designed and published knitting patterns and books.

Throughout all that she's always wanted to be a writer, and she's finally put all her type A, soft-spoken, invisible middle-aged woman focus on that goal, writing everything from fantasy to science fiction, mysteries and romance.

She has sold stories to Pulphouse Magazine and the WMG Holiday Spectacular.

www.stephannietallent.com

Sign up for my newsletter!
https://www.stephannietallent.com/subscribe/

# ALSO BY STEPHANNIE TALLENT

*Short Story Collections*

Gates of Wonder

The Chronicles of Dinah Lee Wright Vol 1

The Chronicles of Dinah Lee Wright Vol 2

Gratitude of the Ocean: Jolene Tomberlin Series

The Serpent in the Shallows: Jolene Tomberlin Series

The Monkey's Journal

The Kaleidoscope Jaguars of the Jungles of Mexicatl

The Mermaid of Ellis Prime

The Alchemy of Science and Mystery

One Plus One Equals More (mystery/crime)

A Snowman Made of Sand (romance)

KnitWitch (fantasy and knitting patterns)